T0197175

PERILOUS TIMES
Life in Post Christian America

Mark A. Hunter

WESTBOW
P R E S S®
A DIVISION OF THOMAS NELSON
& ZONDERVAN

WestBow Press books may be ordered through booksellers or by contacting:

WestBow Press
A Division of Thomas Nelson & Zondervan
1663 Liberty Drive
Bloomington, IN 47403
www.westbowpress.com
1 (866) 928-1240

Because of the dynamic nature of the Internet, any web addresses or
links contained in this book may have changed since publication and may
no longer be valid. The views expressed in this work are solely those
of the author and do not necessarily reflect the views of the publisher,
and the publisher hereby disclaims any responsibility for them.

Any people depicted in stock imagery provided by Getty Images are
models, and such images are being used for illustrative purposes only.
Certain stock imagery © Getty Images.

Scripture taken from the King James Version of the Bible.

ISBN: 978-1-9736-6536-6 (sc)
ISBN: 978-1-9736-6537-3 (hc)
ISBN: 978-1-9736-6535-9 (e)

Library of Congress Control Number: 2019907034

Print information available on the last page.

WestBow Press rev. date: 07/01/2019

For the persecuted church around the world *and* in America

CONTENTS

Acknowledgments ix

Introduction xi

Part I   1

Chapter 1   Postmodern Times 3

Chapter 2   Higher Education 9

Chapter 3   Big Mouth on Campus 15

Chapter 4   Dream Date 20

Chapter 5   A Modest Proposal 25

Chapter 6   Let Them Eat Cake 30

Chapter 7   It's Only Fitting 35

Chapter 8   Alterations 41

Chapter 9   Jack's Back 47

Chapter 10 Bridal Enthusiasm 52

Chapter 11 Pregnant Pause 57

Chapter 12 A Maid of Honor Dishonored 62

Chapter 13 From Perversion to Conversion 67

Chapter 14 Arrested Development 72

Chapter 15 Lawyered Up 77

Chapter 16 The State of Minnesota v. Allison Holtz 82

Chapter 17 Star Witness for the Prosecution 88

Chapter 18 Can I Get a Witness? 93

Chapter 19 Christian Testimony 100

Chapter 20 Sober Judgment 107

Chapter 21 Special Delivery 114

Part II **117**

Chapter 22 Red Headed Blackmailer 119
Chapter 23 Ill-Conceived 123
Chapter 24 Sleeping (Over) with the Enemy 128
Chapter 25 Josefiend 132
Chapter 26 Not Turning the Other Cheek 136
Chapter 27 Déjà Vu All Over Again.. 141
Chapter 28 Fit to Be Tried.. 146
Chapter 29 Grand Perjury 151
Chapter 30 Bearing False Witness 156
Chapter 31 Defenseless.. 160
Chapter 32 Arguments and Apologies 165
Chapter 33 Stuck in Prairie Prison.. 170
Chapter 34 I've Been Working on the (Underground)
            Railroad 175
Chapter 35 Emancipation Proclamation 181
Chapter 36 A Brand-New Saint.. 186
Chapter 37 Euphoria 191
Chapter 38 Dr. McAllister, I Presume 196
Chapter 39 When the Parole Is Called Up Yonder 201
Chapter 40 Give Me Twelve Steps 205
Chapter 41 Genuine Repentance 210
Chapter 42 Rehabitual Liar.. 215
Chapter 43 Unexpectedly Expecting..220
Chapter 44 Abort the Abortion 225
Chapter 45 From Here to Maternity 230
Chapter 46 Epilogue
            The Children of Obedience 238

ACKNOWLEDGMENTS

Thanks to Deb Stortvedt for providing (unpaid) editorial assistance.

INTRODUCTION

The following story, a dystopian satire of a progressive, postmodern, post-Christian culture, takes place in the foreseeable future.

> This know also, that in the last days perilous times shall come. For men shall be lovers of their own selves, covetous, boasters, proud, blasphemers, disobedient to parents, unthankful, unholy, without natural affection, trucebreakers, false accusers, incontinent, fierce, despisers of those that are good, traitors, heady, high-minded, lovers of pleasures more than lovers of God.
>
> —Timothy 3:1–4
> (The second epistle of Paul the apostle to Timothy)

PART I

DEFENDANT OF THE FAITH

We ought to obey God rather than men.

—Acts 5:29

But sanctify the Lord God in your hearts: and
be ready always to give an answer to every man
that asketh you a reason of the hope that is in
you with meekness and fear.

—1 Peter 3:15

CHAPTER 1

Postmodern Times

Allison "Allie" McAllister was eighteen years and seven months old. She was only five foot five at a time when the average height for women was five foot nine. Her red hair hung halfway down her back, and she had freckles and pretty pale-green eyes. The shade of Allie's hair was commonly referred to as red, but most people thought it was closer to orange. Today was a special day for Allie: her high school graduation.

Allie McAllister had just barely graduated from Barack Obama High School. Allie was a good student, but her poor academic performance was a result of her avowed refusal to tow the line on the Common Core, evolutionist, revisionist, morally relativistic, politically correct curriculum. Thus, her schoolwork garnered her C's and D's, whereas most students earned A's and B's for the same quality of work.

Eventually, Allie had learned to couch the answers on her exams with such phrases as "according to the reading materials provided," "Darwin's theory proposed," and the like. But even with these safeguards in place, Allie's subterfuge did not go wholly undetected by her teachers. Near the end of her final semester, her advanced biology instructor, Ms. Nye, a tall, plump woman with long blonde hair, a round face, and eyeglasses, bade Allie to stand up in front of the entire class.

"Ms. McAllister, why must you insist on wording your answers in thoroughly ambiguous ways?" Ms. Nye asked.

"I have—er—relayed the information as it was taught to me in class, even going so far as to cite the correct sources," Allie argued as she stood by her desk.

"As you always do, without fail. But I never quite feel that I am making an impression upon your misguided belief system. Dispensing information is not the only reason for education."

"I'm sorry, Ms. Nye. You may be able to control the content of the material, but you *cannot* force me to believe it."

"In other words, I can lead a horse to water, but I cannot make her think."

This play on words garnered some guffaws from Ms. Nye's biology class.

"I'm afraid not, Ms. Nye," Allie answered resolutely.

"If you insist on continuing to believe in fairy tales rather than in empirical scientific data," Ms. Nye said with a sigh, "then there's not much more I can do."

"Yes, Ms. Nye," Allie answered. She always tried to be polite with people, even those with whom she disagreed.

"You may sit back down, Ms. McAllister."

A relieved Allie complied and took her assigned seat.

At Allie's large high school, there were far too many graduating students to hold a commencement ceremony— it would have taken several hours to complete—so each graduating student was faxed a copy of his or her diploma.

The absence of a commencement ceremony removed the

pomp and circumstance of a high school graduation. Progressive society was nothing if not pragmatic.

But earning a high school diploma was still an achievement, and that was cause for at least some celebration. So Mrs. Billie McAllister, a tall, slender woman with long strawberry-blonde hair, threw her youngest child a graduation party. Of course, Allie's older brother, Rod (who was tall, athletically built, and also strawberry-blond), was there, and all of Allie's friends were there as well. This basically meant her best friend from middle school onward, Cynthia Ann Lake.

Thoroughly postmodern Cindy was everything that Allie was not: a syncretist, a staunch feminist, and an advocate for political correctness in all its various forms. She was the very model of a progressive, postmodern society. Cindy was the same height as Allie; she possessed a slender build and had short, dark-blonde hair, gray eyes, and fair skin. Once the festivities were over, Cindy managed to get Allie alone in Allie's bedroom for a heart-to-heart talk.

"Thank you for coming to my grad party," Allie said as she sat on her bed.

"Don't mention it, Allie Cat," Cindy said. She sat in the computer chair at Allie's desk. "Besides, I have an ulterior motive for being here."

"What do you mean?"

"I'm here to save you."

"But I'm *already* saved."

"I don't mean 'saved' in the Christian sense of the word. I meant that I want to save you from yourself—and from this fanaticism you've bought into."

"You're *not* going to change my mind on what I believe," Allie answered firmly.

"Probably not. But I don't understand *why* you insist on

following that outdated, narrow-minded, old-time religion of Christianity! It really is disgraceful."

"You have a strange concept of what constitutes as 'disgraceful,'" Allie observed.

"Not half as strange as you do."

Allie played along. "So what do you propose I believe in?"

"Why don't you come with me to *my* church sometime, the Worldwide Church of Syncretism? Then you could get in touch with your inner Christ-Krishna-Buddha consciousness, and you'd truly know that *all* religions are one."

"But that's not the gospel!" Allie exclaimed.

"The 'gospel' is politically incorrect, racist, sexist, homophobic claptrap," Cindy contended, quoting the party line of her church and the progressive, postmodern powers that be.

"Those are only distortions of the gospel. The *true* gospel is that Jesus Christ came to save sinners."

"I can't fathom how a smart girl like you still believes in that outmoded concept of racial guilt before God! The only real sin is ignorance of one's true divinity."

"Only God Himself is divine," Allie corrected her friend.

Cindy sighed. "My poor, misguided friend, no sane person believes in that nonsense anymore. But I haven't told you the good news yet!"

"What good news?"

"Acting on your behalf, I took the liberty of arranging to have my minister, Ms. Shirley, pay you a visit to explain the true religion of Syncretism more fully."

"You didn't!" Allie cried. "Cindy, how could you?"

"Now don't get your nun's habit all bunched up, Allie Cat. The least that you can do is to hear Ms. Shirley out."

"Fine, but there is nothing that she or you can say that is *ever* going to make me forsake my devotion to Jesus Christ."

"Nobody said that you have to give up Jesus. *I* believe in Jesus—as a prophet, an avatar, and a good moral teacher. And I believe in Mohammad, Krishna, Buddha, and—"

"They can't *all* be true," Allie interrupted. "Can't you see how every one of these divergent beliefs contradicts each other?"

Cindy solemnly quoted from her church's doctrinal statement. "All religions are one."

"But Jesus Christ said, 'I am the way, the truth, and the life: no man cometh unto the Father, but by Me,'" Allie said, quoting from John 14:6 in the Holy Bible.

"Don't be so narrow-minded and exclusive," Cindy answered.

"'Narrow is the way which leadeth unto life, and few there be that find it,'" Allie said, quoting from Matthew 7:14.

"Even your own religion teaches about both the universal fatherhood of God and our own divinity. 'There is one Father of *all*' that supports universalism, who is *through* all'—that means that everything is God—'and *in* you all'—that means that *everyone* is God," Cindy said, gleefully relaying the World Wide Church of Syncretism's misinterpretation and misquoting of Ephesians 4:6.

"Why didn't you quote the rest of that passage?" Allie asked.

"What 'rest' of the passage?" Cindy asked. "That's correct, as far as I know. Anyway, that's how my church always quotes it."

"Well, your church has it all wrong! The correct passage is, 'There is one body, and one Spirit, even as ye are called in one hope of your calling; one Lord, one faith, one baptism, one God and Father of all, who is above all, and through all, and in you all,'" Allie said, quoting Ephesians 4:4–6 correctly. Then she slyly added, "That sounds pretty exclusive to me!"

"Oh, you're simply impossible! I give up on you, Allie Cat!"

Cindy huffed as she abruptly stood up and stormed out of Allie's bedroom.

"So long, Cindy," Allie said, inwardly pleased that her friend had given up on her.

After Cindy left, there was a knock on Allie's bedroom door.

"Come in," Allie said.

Allie's mother entered the room. "Cindy sure left here in a hurry."

"Apparently Cindy considers me a lost cause as far thinking progressively."

"I, for one, am glad that you have held on to your convictions. And I'm very proud to be the parent of a high school graduate," Billie McAllister declared.

"Thanks, Mom," Allie replied as she gave her mother a big hug.

CHAPTER 2

Higher Education

Allison Jane McAllister was born and raised in a middle-class neighborhood in the city that once was known as Saint Paul, Minnesota. Progressive society had long since removed all vestiges of the religious heritage of the United States of America, including all offending place names. Thus, it now sported the moniker of Darwin City. Other cities in Minnesota also were changed from names of saints to scientists, like Saint Francis (now known as Huxleyville) and Saint Joseph (renamed Dawkinsburg).

By and large, most of the intelligentsia in the United States were Darwinists and atheists, particularly the people who ran the country. Religion was largely seen as, in the words of Karl Marx, "the opiate of the people" or as a subversive force. But Christianity was not yet illegal; Christians were allowed to practice their faith, provided they kept it within the confines of a church building, didn't proselytize, and didn't discriminate against gays, transsexuals, or Muslims.

The McAllister clan consisted of Allie's widowed mother, Billie, who worked as a certified public accountant—Allie's father had died of cancer when she was twelve—and her older brother, Rod. Rod McAllister Jr. was now twenty-one years old and attended a local junior college. His eyes were pale gray, like his father's.

Billie Jo O'Brien was raised in a family with no interest in Christianity. She grew up in a suburb of Minneapolis called Prairie, formally known as Eden Prairie, until the progressive-minded civic leaders dropped the biblically inspired part of the name. She was a good student and a popular girl with a great sense of humor. After high school, she studied accountancy at the local university and worked as a waitress in a Minneapolis dive known as the Gopher Diner.

Billie met Rod McAllister when she began doing the books for him. Rod was a computer programmer for a major corporation in Minneapolis, and he also ran a home business on the side called WebDesign; he designed websites for small and/or home businesses. At that time, Billie was an attractive twentysomething; Rod was big and burly, with red hair and a bristly red beard to match. He was recently divorced at the time, and he and Billie dated tentatively at first, but the relationship grew stronger and eventually led to marriage.

Rod McAllister's second marriage was successful, lasting until his untimely death from bone cancer. While he was fighting his losing battle with cancer, Rod, who was as unchurched as his wife, began to contemplate his own mortality. He researched various religions, and before he passed on, as a result of reading the New Testament, he concluded that Christianity was the one true religion.

The Holy Bible had been banned in schools about one hundred years after prayer was removed, and it had been removed from the shelves of any public library, but Bibles were still legal in churches and homes. They still were obtainable, if one was inclined to find one, and Mrs. McAllister found a dilapidated copy of the New Testament in a used-book store in the city formally known as Saint Paul. She bought it and brought it to her dying husband.

After Rod's death, Billie began to read the New Testament for herself, and by the time she'd read through the Gospel of John, she also had accepted Jesus Christ as her personal Lord and Savior. Neither of her children had a positive opinion of a God who had let their beloved father die. But eventually, they both stopped hating their heavenly Father long enough to listen to what their earthly mother had to say about Him. Allie got saved first, and then rebellious teenager Rod Jr. finally succumbed as well.

The only guiding light the McAllister family had possessed since then was that well-worn copy of the New Testament. For the first few years following their conversions, the McAllisters were not even aware that an Old Testament existed (much less knowing where to buy one), but they finally found an ancient copy of the entire Holy Bible in that same used-book store called Second-Hand News.

Most of the true Christian churches had long since been closed down by the government or sued out of existence for refusing to perform gay weddings; ditto the Christian schools and Bible colleges that refused to admit practicing homosexuals and transgenders. All that remained were the liberal churches that spoke about social causes and eschewed teaching or preaching from the Holy Bible—or even mentioning it.

Allie had tried attending those churches, but she could only stand hearing "God is love" and "Judge not, lest ye be judged" (always taken out of context) for so long before she would leave in disgust. She had to rely on the fellowship of her immediate family instead. Thus, the McAllister family operated a home church of three, flying under the radar of the watchful eyes of the US government. As a result, Miss McAllister had long labored under the assumption that she and her family might have been the only Christians left alive (or at least the only ones still in their immediate area).

Allie had tried to witness to her friends (most of whom she lost as friends as a result), including Cindy Lake. One evening as the two of them hung out in Allie's bedroom, Allie shared her faith, but her words fell on deaf ears:

"Who are you, and what have you done with Allie McAllister?" Cindy asked.

"I realize that I've changed a lot since my conversion to Christ," Allie admitted, "but I meant what I said. God's forgiveness is available to everyone."

"Sorry, Al Pal, but I don't feel like being preached at right now."

"I understand. No more preaching; I promise. But would you at least consider what I've told you?"

"Okay, but I really have no interest in such a politically incorrect religion as Christianity. I'm much happier attending my grandparents' church: the Worldwide Church of Syncretism, Darwin City branch."

Allie did not lose Cindy as a friend, but neither did she gain a convert.

Allie had always been a reasonably attractive girl, and she easily could have acquired a boyfriend, but she wanted a Christian boyfriend, and that was something in short supply. Thus, she had long ago given up meeting the fine, young, Christian man of her romantic dreams.

But while Allie was a staunch Christian, she was also human. She couldn't help noticing the more attractive members of the opposite gender; she even entertained the occasional schoolgirl crush on some of them from time to time. But what good did it do her? She knew that she was forbidden to be unequally yoked with an unbeliever.

Having graduated from high school at eighteen, Allie had set her mind on higher education. She was of above-average intelligence (no matter what her grades indicated), and she knew that she wanted to do more with her life than simply work in a diner like her mother had. Obviously, what she wanted most of all was to be a wife and mother. But, as the saying goes, it takes two to tango, and so far, she hadn't found anyone to tango *with*.

But thanks to Allie's poor grades, poor ASAT scores (due to her refusal to regurgitate Common Core nonsense on the test), and unorthodox religious views (duly noted on her permanent record), she knew that she could forget attending most colleges, especially the Ivy League schools back East (many of which, ironically enough, had started out as Christian institutions). The best that she could hope for now was acceptance at one of the many local junior colleges, which had the lowest academic requirements anywhere.

Providentially, Miss McAllister was able to find a nearby junior college in Edina that cared more about making money than in turning out doctors, lawyers, and MBAs. The chief advantage was that the school was close enough that Allie could commute back and forth from home instead of living on campus. All college dorms nationwide were coed, and Allie was afraid of meeting a male student (or perhaps several male students at once) who wouldn't take no for an answer.

She was thankful to have dodged that particular bullet, and Allie happily started college the next autumn. Edina Community College was small, intimate, and located well within driving distance. Allie fully expected that the professors would be even harder on her than her high school teachers had been, and she steeled herself for the potentially negative experience. On the morning of Allie's first day of college, Billie Jo McAllister bade her daughter farewell.

"You keep holding on to your Christian principles, and don't let those godless professors shipwreck your faith."

"I won't," Allie vowed.

"And stay away from wild parties and from drugs … and from all boys, unless he is truly a Christian," Mrs. McAllister warned.

"I'll be a good girl, Mom. I promise."

"Then off you go," Billie Jo said as she hugged her youngest child tightly. "I'll pray for you."

"Fervently, I hope," Allie said as she kissed her mother on the cheek and then excitedly exited the house.

CHAPTER 3

Big Mouth on Campus

At the tender age of eighteen, Allie McAllister resolved to remain single for the rest of her life, if need be, unless God, in His infinite wisdom, saw fit to bring the right guy into that life. Although Allie was a Christian girl, however, she definitely was not blind; thus she could not help but notice a rather good-looking young man around campus. He was of average height and well-formed in both face and body, and the T-shirts he often wore displayed muscular biceps.

Allie saw him five days a week, going to and from classes, and when she did, she noticed that he always moved quickly, like a man on a mission. Whenever they happened to pass each other in the halls or on the walkways between buildings, he would give her a slight smile or a nod of his head. Allie would venture a shy smile in return, but that was all that she could manage. She desperately tried not to fall head over heels in love with the big man on campus, but that wasn't easy!

Allie soon found that she wasn't the only female student who had noticed the lad. Allie usually didn't use public restrooms—since the passage of the Transgender Law, she was uncomfortable with sharing the facilities with males— but necessity demanded it one particular day. She was in the women's restroom in the academic building when she overheard a couple of young ladies talking to each other as they primped and preened in front of the restroom mirrors.

"Have you seen that good-looking freshman—Jack Holtz?" one girl asked the other.

"What does he look like?" the other young lady asked.

The first speaker described Jack Holtz in minute anatomical detail, and Allie was sure that the young lady was describing her mystery man. So now she had a name to go with the handsome face. But she wondered why, if he was a freshman, she didn't have any classes with him. She had previously figured that he must be an upperclassman—or upperclassperson, to be politically correct—while she was but a lowly freshman.

"Oh, yeah, I certainly have noticed him," the second person said with enthusiasm. "What a dreamboat!"

"Yeah … but unfortunately, he's also a whole boatload of crazy!" the first person said.

"What do you mean?"

"He's got all of these kooky religious ideas. He's always arguing with the profs about something. Do you know what the other students call him? Big mouth on campus!"

The two young ladies giggled riotously.

"I get it; instead of big man on campus!" The other girl laughed. "Honestly though, I'd be happy to put up with his kooky religious ideas, if only he would use his big mouth on *me*!"

"The problem is, he's probably the type who would insist on matrimony first."

With that, the two ladies left the restroom together. Allie's head was spinning. Could this Jack Holtz be her long-sought-after Christian young man? But Allie tried not to get her hopes up too much; she didn't want to be disappointed again. Besides, she didn't want to be so lost in thought that she got caught alone in a public restroom. She just managed to get her hands washed and dried before a male student entered, and she had to make a hasty retreat.

Following the winter break—not Christmas break; progressive society would never use a word with Christ in it— Allie began the second semester of her freshman year. One of her required classes was History of Western Civilization. Western Civ was required for all students, including transfer students, even if they had already taken a similar class somewhere else.

On the first day of class, Allie took a seat at random and quickly discovered that she was seated right next to Jack Holtz—roll call confirmed that was his name. Allie tried not to look at him too much during class and not to think about him too much while away from class. She didn't know for certain that Jack was a fellow Christian, and she had no desire to encourage an attraction that could be doomed to failure.

History of Western Civilization mostly reiterated the litany of the exploitive abuses perpetrated by white, imperialistic Christian males toward Native Americans, African Americans, women, homosexuals, and transgenders. It was the same sort of rhetoric that Allie had heard for her entire scholastic life. Of course, she didn't agree that everything the professor branded as abuse actually constituted as such, and if it did, she wasn't sure that Christians were always the culprits.

But Allie kept her head down, her mouth shut, and her right hand busily scribbling copious lecture notes. During class one day, Jack began to argue with the professor, and Allie was really surprised by how well-constructed his arguments were. The freshman (or fresh*person*, to keep with the college's politically correct policies) even cited precedent and source material that Allie had never heard of because most of the material had been banned years ago.

From that day forward, Jack was a marked man. Professor Kirk (tall, thin, and balding) was on him during every single class, attempting (but usually failing) to poke holes in Holtz's cogent arguments. Jack always stood his ground, pointing out that Christians were at the forefront of many humanitarian efforts (like hospitals and orphanages), as well as being pioneers in education and the sciences.

"The *sciences*?" Professor Kirk repeated in disbelief. "It was the Christian Church that persecuted scientists like Galileo and Copernicus!"

"Actually, it was the Roman Catholic Church, *not* Christians, who persecuted Galileo and Copernicus," Jack countered.

"What's the difference?" Professor Kirk demanded in exasperation.

"Scientists like Galileo and Copernicus and Sir Isaac Newton were all Christians. The scientific method was developed by believers in God who also believed that the universe displayed an orderliness that could have *only* come from a Creator—that is, until Darwin came up with his spurious theory of evolution."

"If you are too stupid to accept the fact of evolution, then I believe this 'spurious' discussion is at an end," Professor Kirk haughtily replied.

Allie was impressed by Jack's knowledge and courage but also with his demeanor. Jack never once lost his temper, which was more than she could say for his adversary. While Jack quite humbly never denied the white man's part in the atrocities committed against the African and Native American races, he never once admitted that true Christians were involved.

One day, when the subject of slavery was discussed, Jack

once again interrupted the professor. "Every culture has practiced slavery, even African cultures, from ancient times," Jack argued. "The Christians didn't start slavery, but the Christians ended it—Christians like William Wilberforce, who battled in Parliament for nearly fifty years to end slavery in England, and finally succeeded when he was on his deathbed."

"Wilberforce?" Professor Kirk scoffed "Even the name sounds made up!"

This denouncement won Professor Kirk some points from his class, but Allie was sure that if Jack Holtz said it, it was true *and* that he had the sources to back it up. Jack's actions and opinions didn't win him many friends among the faculty or his fellow classmates, but he definitely gained at least one fan at Edina Community College.

After class that day, Allie put aside her natural timidity, sidled up to Jack, and whispered, "I've agreed with everything that you've said in class so far."

CHAPTER 4

Dream Date

Following Allie's admission, she and Jack began conversing with each other on a regular basis. They soon found that they were of one accord on myriad issues—politics, religion, creation versus evolution, political correctness, and morals in general. Allie found it refreshing to finally find someone of like mind after so many years; other than her immediate family, she had felt isolated for so long. And the fact that this someone was so easy on the eyes was a definite plus.

As much as they may have had in common, however, their backgrounds were strikingly dissimilar. John David Holtz—nicknamed Jack—was born and raised in the Midwestern state of Nebraska in a Christian home. The Holtz family had been Christians for generations, from time out of mind. Jack began his formal learning by being homeschooled, until the federal government outlawed homeschooling.

Yet even after he had been indoctrinated for years by the government-run school system, Jack still held on to his Christian beliefs and principles. Upon graduating from high school, Jack joined the army for a five-year hitch, which was how he ended up in Minnesota, having been stationed there. Jack realized early on that with his religious views, he would not rise very far in the military, so he served his five years and then left with an honorable discharge.   Now Jack was attending college on the GI Bill and serving in the US Army Reserve.

Allie was correct in guessing that Jack was older than she was, even though he was a fellow freshman. Jack Holtz was starting out his college career at the relatively late age of twenty-three, and he was certainly starting it out with a bang (though decidedly not with the big bang).

During the second week of February, while Allie was sitting in the student lounge, Jack walked quickly and determinedly over to her and said, "Hi, Allie, how's it going?"

"It's all right. No major instances of being called on the carpet in front of the entire class today," Allie answered.

"That's good," Jack said, but he seemed distracted.

Allie could tell that he had something more to say, and she waited for him to say it.

"You know, Allie," Jack began tentatively, "the two of us have so much in common, so I was wondering …"

"You were wondering *what?*" Allie prompted him encouragingly. She hoped she didn't sound as impatient as she felt.

"I was wondering if you would like to go out on a date."

Allie found Jack's demeanor cute, even comical. She also found it surprising. Jack Holtz was one of the best-looking guys on campus; girls were always after him and throwing themselves at him.

Jack could have any girl he wants, Allie thought. *Why would he want an average-looking girl like me?* Allie couldn't understand why Jack was asking her out in the first place, much less why he was so nervous about it.

Jack was more interested in a lasting relationship than in a one-night stand. He was interested in a lasting relationship with a good Christian girl like Allison Jane McAllister.

It took a while for Allie to stop contemplating the situation and respond to his question. "Um, okay," Allie answered with a shrug of her freckle-covered shoulders.

Allie sounded nonchalant, but inwardly, she was jumping for joy. She had been waiting for a day like this for what seemed her entire life (although it actually only was the past six years or so). She had never been asked out by a Christian before, one she felt she could trust to respect her dedication to preserve her virginity until marriage. Having agreed to the date, Allie then inquired, "When would you like to go out?"

"How about the fourteenth?" Jack suggested.

"February the fourteenth?" Allie gasped. "As in Cupid's Day?"

February 14 once had been known as Saint Valentine's Day. The name had long since been changed, for the obvious reason, but the holiday still existed as a celebration of romantic love. Allie figured if Jack wanted to take her out on Cupid's Day, he must really be serious about her.

"Yes, Cupid's Day. As for where I'm taking you, it's a surprise."

For her dream date, Allie got all dressed in her Sunday best: a pastel green (to match her eye color), full-length silk gown, white pumps, and the requisite winter coat. She was so nervous! Finally, after what seemed like forever, Jack arrived in his very used sedan and sped them off to his chosen destination: Jake's Fake Steakhouse. Meat-eating had long since been outlawed by most countries, so synthetic meat was the closest to the real thing for any law-abiding citizen who possessed carnivorous inclinations.

Owing to the holiday, the place was packed. But thanks to Jack's having made reservations, the two of them were shown to a table immediately (even though it was the table closest to the kitchen). The opulence of the place surprised Allie, as did her date, who gallantly opened doors for her and pulled out her chair—Jack was trying to impress her. As they feasted on the fake steak and other fine cuisine, they discussed their mutual backgrounds and belief systems.

"I honestly thought that I was the only Christian left," Allie said. "Me and my immediate family, that is."

"I often thought that too," Jack agreed, "only it was me and my extended family and a few other families in Nebraska. Perhaps God has reserved for Himself seven thousand in America whose knees have not bowed to Darwin."

"Maybe," Allie answered, "but I strongly suspect that most of the remnant is *not* located up here in Minnesota."

After their dream date, Jack took Allie home, where she found her mother sitting on the living room sofa, waiting up for her.

"How was your date?" Mrs. McAllister asked eagerly.

Allie collapsed on the sofa next to her mother and sighed. "It was wonderful!"

"Except for the food, I suspect."

"The food was fine, Mom. We had a most delicious meal of synthetic steak."

"You wouldn't say that if you'd ever had *real* steak," Mrs. McAllister said, although she could just barely recall the taste of authentic meat from her childhood. "He didn't try anything, did he?"

"Jack was the perfect gentleman," Allie said.

"Then perhaps this boy really is a Christian."

"I sure hope so," Allie said wistfully.

Jack Holtz had better be a Christian boy, she thought, *because I'm falling head over heels in love with him!*

CHAPTER 5

A Modest Proposal

Not too many days after their date, Jack asked Allie out again, she said yes again, and they went out on another date. This ritual was often repeated until the two of them were officially an item. This fact did not stop the other female students at Edina Community College from shamelessly throwing themselves at Jack, often right in front of Allie. One of Jack's most persistent admirers was a peroxide-blonde beauty named Molly Malone.

Allie was pretty sure that Molly had been the second speaker during that conversation in the girl's restroom last semester. Molly was always trailing after them and propositioning Jack. One day, Molly was doggedly following them, as usual, as they walked down the sidewalk hand in hand. She suddenly ran ahead of them, planted herself right in front of them, put her hands upon her hips, and stated in no uncertain terms, "I want you, Jack Holtz, and I won't take no for an answer."

"But I already have a girlfriend," Jack replied simply.

"C'mon, Jack, why would you want *her* when you could have *me*?"

"Hey!" Allie cried. "I'm standing right here, ya know."

"I'm quite happy with my gal," Jack answered, and he kissed Allie on the cheek.

The young couple walked past Jack's would-be seductress, leaving her flat-footed.

By the end of their freshman year, the relationship was serious enough for Allie to bring her beau home to meet the family. Mrs. McAllister fixed Jack's favorite dish, pizza (sans real meat, in accordance with the government's directive on vegetarianism). A pleasant meal was had by one and all.

During the dinner, Mrs. McAllister asked Jack, "How did you become a Christian, John?" (Billie Jo always insisted on using Jack's proper name.)

"When I was four years old, I was afraid of going to hell, so my mother explained how I could avoid going there by accepting Jesus Christ as my personal Savior."

"I'm surprised that you can remember the conversion or that you understood what you were doing at that young age."

"I'm sure that I didn't understand all of the aspects of the gospel back then, Mrs. McAllister, but you know what Jesus Christ said about having the faith of a child."

"Your background is so different from ours, John," Billie McAllister observed. "I didn't become a Christian until I was nearly forty years old!"

"It's never too early or too late to get saved," he replied pleasantly.

Later, after Jack had left, Allie asked her mother, "What did you think of Jack?"

"I think he's definitely a keeper," Allie's mama replied.

Following that dinner, Jack was a welcome visitor at the McAllister home. Young Mr. Holtz proved to be a good role model for Allie's brother on what an articulate Christian man looked and sounded like. Rod Jr., who was now twenty-two years old and a graduate of Edina Community College, had long ago become a closet Christian. But Jack's brave example emboldened Rod to live out his faith for the first time in his life.

Allie and Jack both had managed to pass all of their classes, and their romance continued unabated during that summer. The following October, in honor of Allie's twentieth birthday, Jack took Allie to what had become "their" place— Jake's Fake Steakhouse. After another fine dinner of artificial steak, Jack got down on bended knee, pulled out a small jewelry box, and presented Allie with a diamond engagement ring, as he uttered the following words: "Allison Jane McAllister, will you marry me?"

Allie simply stared at the band of gold with the gorgeous (albeit tiny) diamond set in it; she was absolutely mute. She had waited for this moment for years, never daring to hope that the moment would arrive. When she finally found her voice, she managed to whisper *yes.* Jack then placed the ring on Allie's left ring finger and stood up. Allie threw her arms around her intended's neck and planted a multitude of kisses upon his lips. She knew that she was making a scene (marriage proposals had become rare, especially *public* marriage proposals), but she hardly cared a fig about that at the moment.

"I realize that it's not a very large ring," Jack said, "and we probably won't be able to afford the grandest of weddings—"

"It's the most beautiful engagement ring I've ever seen," Allie murmured as she gazed at it, transfixed. "And don't worry about the expense of our wedding. I've been saving up for my wedding day for years."

After Allie bestowed another round of kisses on her beau, Jack attempted to bring her back down to earth by saying, "But I only make a modest salary in the Reserve, and I cannot exactly promise you a life of ease."

"I grew up middle class, so I'm used to not exactly being a rich girl," Allie reassured her future husband. "What *will* take some getting used to is the idea of being married to the Christian man of my dreams."

Many more kisses ensued.

After Jack's proposal, he took a giddily happy Allie back home. As soon as she entered the house, she proudly showed off her engagement ring to her family.

"Look, Ma," Allie excitedly exclaimed as she flashed her left hand in front of her mother's face.

Mrs. McAllister stood in front of the kitchen sink, washing the supper dishes. "An engagement ring?" Billie Jo McAllister gasped.

"*What* engagement ring?" Rod joked as he sat at the kitchen table and squinted at the small rock on his sister's finger. "Where's the diamond, Allie Cat?"

Allie frowned.

"Don't listen to your brother, Allison," Mrs. McAllister countered. "*I* think that it's a lovely ring. It's not the size of the ring that matters; it's the size of the heart of the man who presented it to you."

"Thank you, Mama," Allie replied as she hugged her mother. Then she turned toward her elder brother, stuck her tongue out at him, and said, "So there!"

During the winter break from classes, Jack was invited over to the McAllisters' home for the first Christmas that he was spending away from his home. Progressive society had long ago rolled all of the winter holidays (Christmas, Hanukkah, and Kwanzaa) into the Winter Solstice Season, so as to not offend any atheists.

The McAllisters and their guest were the only people in the area who celebrated the true meaning of Christmas. It wasn't a holiday the McAllisters had observed before their conversions. Mrs. McAllister had been only vaguely aware of Christmas or Christianity while growing up. She had developed an interest in knowing God only after the death of her husband (which is why, when she had come across the New Testament in that used-book store, she bought it more for her husband than for herself).

Allie set up the Nativity scene, which she'd bought at a thrift store, and after Jack taught them the words to Christmas carols, they all sang together.

Chapter 6

Let Them Eat Cake

Allie set about to bring her cherished adolescent dreams of her wedding day to fruition. She had been squirreling away money from her waitressing job at the Gopher Diner (where she had followed in her mother's flat-heeled footsteps some twenty years later) for years and had amassed quite the nest egg. Added to this treasure was an offer of financial help from her future in-laws; not having a daughter of their own, they were more than happy to aid in the process of losing a son to gain a daughter.

But Mrs. Holtz was not geographically near enough to Allie to contribute much more than her money, and even Mrs. McAllister was too busy to help much. Furthermore, the husband-to-be was soon to be taken completely out of the picture. The United States of America had become entangled in the latest chapter of the continuing war on terror when the newest radical Muslim terrorist group reared its ugly (turban-covered) head, and Jack's unit was deployed to the Middle East to combat it.

"I can't believe that I've *finally* found you, and now you're being taken away from me!" A tearful Allie cried on the shoulder of her intended, as she tightly hugged him goodbye before he departed for the military base.

"God will take care of both of us," Jack reminded his betrothed. "But if worse comes to worst, we will meet again in heaven, where we will be together forever. And then no one will be able to take me away from you ever again."

With Jack gone, Allie was left to do most of the wedding arrangements by herself. The first step was applying for a marriage license. Allie drove down to the Hennepin County Clerk's office to apply. So few people even bothered to be legally wed these days that obtaining a wedding license had become anachronistic, but there were still enough applicants to justify having a lone clerk employed for such purposes. The clerk, a woman in her late thirties with short, light-brown hair, sat down with Allie to ask perfunctory questions.

"When is the proposed date of the wedding?" she asked.

"July 1 of this year, provided my betrothed can get leave from the military around that date."

"And are you the bride or the groom?"

"Oh, the bride, of course," Allie answered matter-of-factly, somewhat surprised by the question.

"Thank you," the clerk answered. Then, in response to Allie's obvious confusion, she added, "You never can tell these days—believe me. And your full name, please?"

"Allison—with two L's—Jane McAllister."

"And do you prefer the designation of Ms., Mr., or neither?"

"I prefer 'Miss,' or at least I will until I'm married. Then I'll be Mrs."

"And what is the name or names of the groom and/or

grooms or the other bride and/or brides who are to be involved in this marriage?"

"There is only *one* groom—and only one bride, for that matter," Allie said.

"A *traditional* marriage, eh? We don't get many of those anymore. And what is this groom's name, please?"

"Jack—er, actually his Christian name is John. John David Holtz."

"His *Christian* name?" the clerk asked with raised eyebrows.

"I meant his given name," Allie amended.

"Thank Darwin. I was afraid you meant he's one of *those*!"

"Well, if you mean a Christian, then yes, he *is* one of those. We both are."

"Oh," the clerk answered without any attempt to hide the contempt in her voice, "so this is going to be a *Christian* marriage, is it?"

"Yes, ma'am," Allie answered respectfully.

The clerk sniffed. "That's *Ms.* Schultz to you, 'Miss' McAllister."

"Sorry, *Ms.* Schultz," Allie corrected, still attempting to be polite in the face of blatant opposition.

"You are, of course, familiar with the state of Minnesota's laws pertaining to equal access for entities of all races, genders, sexual orientation, religious beliefs (or lack of them), regarding public accommodation, even including wedding ceremonies."

"Anyone is welcome to attend our wedding ceremony," Allie promised.

"Good. Well, seeing as Christianity and Christian marriages are not yet illegal and that you solemnly swear not to discriminate against anyone on the basis of race, gender, or sexual orientation during your wedding ceremony, the county of Hennepin grants your petition to be wed in Minneapolis, Minnesota, on the first day of July of this year."

"Thank you." Allie breathed a sigh of relief as she got up to leave.

Having completed this arduous task, Allie next turned her attention to acquiring a wedding cake. Despite there not being much call for wedding cakes anymore, there was still a multitude of bakeries in the immediate area that catered to birthday parties and other events (including the occasional wedding). The closest one to the county clerk's office was Let Them Eat Cake, located in Minneapolis, so Allie tried there first.

When Allie entered the shop, she heard the bell ring over the door, and then a woman behind the counter said, "Welcome to Let Them Eat Cake—wedding cakes a specialty!" The woman—Cassandra by name—was very big and very tall and had medium-brown hair tied back into a bun. She wore a decorative red-and-white candy-striped apron.

Allie smiled and replied, almost as cheerfully as Cassandra, "That's great, because I'm in need of a wedding cake."

"Then you've certainly come to the right place. Let me show you my creations."

After looking at some absolutely beautiful confectionary delights, Allie picked out a particular design and requested a chocolate cake with the requisite white butter-cream frosting.

Then Cassandra cheerfully said, "Good. Now let's talk cake toppers, shall we?"

She walked behind the counter and opened a large white book that was resting upon it. Within this book were pages of photos displaying every conceivable figurine. There were toppers of two brides, two grooms, two brides and one groom, two grooms and one bride, two grooms *and* two brides, and so on, until Allie had seen so many that she could hardly imagine a wedding cake top wide enough to support them all.

Allie finally asked, "Don't you have any toppers with only one bride and one groom?"

"Ah, a traditional wedding. How quaint! Yes, I suppose that we must have something like that in here somewhere." Cassandra began to rapidly page through the big white book. "I'm afraid we don't get much call for traditional cake toppers anymore," she apologized as she continued to turn pages. Then she abruptly stopped. "Ah! Here we are!" she announced triumphantly, pointing to a photo.

Displayed was a traditional couple—a brown-haired groom proudly standing next to his bride, who was shorter, red-haired, and looking quite demure. Allie gasped loudly.

"You like?" Cassandra asked rhetorically.

"It's perfect!" an excited Allie replied.

"Then it shall be yours. Or it *will* be yours, once I find it in stock or special order it—for a nominal fee, of course."

"Of course," Allie acknowledged.

Allie put in her order for the wedding cake and the perfect cake topper, paid for it, and then left the bakery feeling overjoyed with her success so far.

Chapter 7

It's Only Fitting

Next was shopping for a wedding dress. Allie came across an advert in the phone book that read, "It's Only Fitting Formal Wear: tuxedos, prom dresses, and wedding gowns." The address given was not far from Allie's neighborhood, so she decided to give them a try. She entered the rather posh-looking interior of the place of business and immediately saw a multitude of tuxes and prom dresses, although no wedding gowns and no salesperson.

Eventually, a tall, ravishingly beautiful Asian woman with long, raven-black hair, almond-brown eyes, and high cheekbones came sauntering Allie's way. She was impeccably dressed in a scarlet-velour sleeveless dress, with a skirt that reached her mid-thigh, and high spiked heels. Allie always felt immature and physically inadequate when in the presence of such goddess-like creatures as this woman.

When the goddess in question spoke, her voice betrayed both a blasé attitude and annoyance at having been interrupted in whatever task she had been doing. "Yes?"

"I'm looking for a wedding dress," Allie said.

"For yourself, I assume," she said.

"You should never assume, but in this case, you assume correctly."

"Walk this way." The salesperson, whose name tag read *Tiffany*, sauntered toward the back of the store.

Allie obediently followed, inwardly wishing that she could walk that way, if only her little legs could compete with Tiffany's magnificently long limbs.

"The wedding gowns are located in the rear of the store," Tiffany explained as they walked along. "I'm afraid we don't get much call for them anymore."

I'm getting used to hearing that, Allie thought.

Eventually, they came to a selection of white wedding gowns of nearly every shape, size, and style, although most of the styles showed much more skin than Allie was comfortable displaying in public. Despite the wide selection, though, Tiffany was quite correct when she observed, "Obviously, these gowns are far too long for you unless they are altered."

Fine, just rub it in, why don't ya? Allie thought.

"But if you'll simply come with me, I think that we have just the thing for you." Tiffany then led her customer to an area displaying smaller wedding gowns. "Here is our Child Bride collection," Tiffany announced proudly, with a grand sweep of her right hand.

"But I'm *not* a child—"

"The term 'child bride' is used euphemistically here. It's simply a marketing ploy," Tiffany patiently explained. "Officially speaking, It's Only Fitting does not condone or provide their services for any weddings involving persons under the current legal age of fifteen. Of course, you're obviously not a child. You don't look a day under fifteen years old."

"Actually, I'm twenty years old," Allie said.

With her fresh-faced good looks and the abundance of

freckles on her face, Allie was constantly mistaken for being much younger than she actually was. Allie McAllister also possessed a tidy figure, and though she was by no means drop-dead gorgeous, she was definitely a cutie-pie (strawberry-rhubarb pie, perhaps, considering her hair color, or maybe a cutie carrot cake, owing to her being a carrot top).

"Your intended must be into girls who possess the young look," said Tiffany.

"My future husband loves me for my inner beauty," Allie stated proudly, taking mild umbrage at what Tiffany was implying.

Tiffany smirked. "Yes, but isn't that what they all say?"

Allie chose to ignore Tiffany's further insinuations and instead focused on the wedding gowns. While there was no doubt that the sizes were more appropriate for Allie's smaller frame, the designs once again left too little to the imagination. The manufacturers certainly had not wasted material on these dresses, and the high hemlines, sleeveless arms, and cleavage-revealing low-cut fronts made the gowns look more like the "Child Prostitute" line than the "Child Bride" collection.

"Do you have anything more conservative?" Allie asked.

"Conservative?" Tiffany repeated, scrunching up her nose.

Conservative was a dirty word in her progressive, postmodern society, a fact that Allie constantly forgot.

"I mean a little less ... skimpy?" Allie said.

"Oh! So you really meant conservative because you are, in fact, a conservative. The next thing you're going to tell me is that you're one of those Christians!"

"I *am* one of those Christians!" Allie retorted.

"Seriously? Well, I guess that it takes all kinds."

Allie was becoming more offended by the minute and contemplated storming out of the store altogether.

Then Tiffany said, "You know, I think I might have something back in storage that could work."

Allie decided to give Tiffany the benefit of the doubt and waited impatiently for her to return with the dress. While she waited, Allie prayed that she would find a God-honoring wedding gown, one that wouldn't appeal to the wrong motives of a man (not even *her* man). In some ways, she felt silly for praying for something as frivolous as a wedding dress, but she knew that the Bible commanded that Christians should, by "prayer and supplication," let their requests be known unto God.

Eventually, Tiffany returned with a garment bag. She unzipped the bag and pulled out a small but breathtakingly beautiful, pristine-white wedding gown. This particular gown appeared to leave everything to the imagination. The skirt was full-length, the neckline was high, and the sleeves were long. But the dress was no plain-Jane house frock; it was a stylish silk gown with an embroidered lace pattern covering the arms and the bodice, with a lace flower design on the long skirt.

Allie lovingly gazed at the gown and murmured, "May I try it on?"

"Certainly," Tiffany replied, leading Allie to the dressing rooms.

As she walked toward the dressing room, Allie's euphoric mood was tempered somewhat by her phobia of undressing in public places. Ever since the passage of the Transgender Law, which allowed either gender to use whichever restroom, dressing room, or locker room they wished, Allie felt uptight in these situations, especially as she suspected that many of the men who exercised this option were not so much women trapped in men's bodies as they were typical men who only wanted to ogle women's bodies.

But Allie was too enthralled by the wedding dress to stop

now, so she sent out a quick prayer for her own safety and entered the dressing room and got right down to business. She quickly undressed and slipped into the gown. She had to enlist Tiffany's help to zip it up in back and to fasten the clasp at the back of her neck, but once these tasks were completed, Allie gazed dreamily at her reflection in the full-length mirror.

To her surprise, the gown fit almost perfectly; it was a little too big in the bodice, and the sleeves covered her hands (she wasn't going for the "right to bare arms" look anyway). On the plus side, however, the hemline touched the floor, and it had a high neckline that almost covered her entire neck. In other words, there would be no leg show or skin flicks at her wedding.

"What do you think?" Tiffany asked.

"It's perfect!" Allie pronounced, transfixed by her own reflection.

"No, it's not perfect yet," Tiffany contradicted, "but it will be, once it's been taken in some."

Allie finally managed to take her eyes off the mirror. Beaming, she turned to Tiffany and said, "I'll take it!"

"Excellent choice," Tiffany agreed; then she helped her satisfied customer out of her new purchase.

Once Allie was again in her street clothes, she left the dressing room and settled her bill. She was pleasantly surprised when she learned of the low price.

"To tell you the truth, this gown has been seriously marked down," Tiffany said. "We'd honestly despaired of anyone's ever being interested in buying such modest attire for her wedding day—of all days."

"Believe it or not, this gown is an answer to a prayer," Allie said.

"Oh, so you still follow that religious practice, do you?"

Chapter 8

Alterations

Tiffany's suggestion made Allie contemplate the issue of having bridesmaids at her wedding. While her betrothed had several brothers to choose from for groomsmen, Allie did not enjoy such a luxury regarding bridesmaids. Owing to her unconventional religious views, Allie never had many friends. Her only constant friendship was with Cindy Lake, and even then, they had hardly spoken to each other since Allie's graduation party, nearly two years earlier.

Allie figured that she would be blessed if she could come up with even one bridesmaid, so she decided to settle for a maid of honor only. She briefly considered her own mother as matron of honor, but because her father was deceased, Allie hoped to have her mother give her away. Besides the shortage of friends, Allie longed to mend fences with her once-best friend, so she called her to break the joyous news.

When Cindy answered her cell phone and realized it was Allie, she said, "Al Pal! How's college life treating you?"

"It's fine, but I have some wonderful news. I'm getting married!"

Cindy gasped. "Already? Why are you throwing your life away by getting married at the tender age of twenty-years-old?"

"You actually believe twenty is too young to get married?" Allie asked.

"Well, duh!" Cindy answered. "You have your whole life ahead of you, so why would you want to get married to the first guy you've ever dated? You probably don't even know if you two are compatible."

"I know for a fact that we are very compatible," Allie countered. "Jack shares all of my 'wacko religious views,' as you insist on calling them."

"I'm not talking about that sort of compatibility. I meant physically compatible. I understand that you believe that marriage is a lifelong commitment. Do you really want to commit to someone before you've determined that?"

"You talk like that's the only reason to get married!"

"What other reason is there?" Cindy asked in exasperation.

Allie listed her reasons. "Producing children, showing mutual love and respect for each other, modeling the love that Christ has for His church—"

"What strange views you hold, Allie Cat," Cindy interrupted.

"Listen, Cindy, I didn't call you to engage in a debate. The *real* reason that I called is to ask you to be my maid of honor."

"Really?" Cindy sounded quite touched by the offer, which surprised Allie, but Cindy quickly recovered and said in a superior tone, "I still don't understand why you want to take part in such an antiquated, puritanical, patriarchal institution as marriage, but since you do, I'd be honored to be your maid of honor."

"Thank you, Cindy."

A week later, Allie got a call from It's Only Fitting and made an appointment to pick up her gown. Allie invited Cindy to accompany her, in order to pick out a bridesmaid dress as well.

Allie had chosen pale green (to match her eyes) and pristine white (to match her purity) as her wedding colors, but they found few gowns that were pale green.

Cindy was not about to wear a skimpy, slinky, silky number that looked more like something a bride might wear on her wedding night than what a bridesmaid would wear on the wedding day. She wasn't conservative like Allie, but such risqué attire offended her feminist beliefs. Unlike Cindy's fashion-model mother, Cindy had no interest in a modeling career. Cindy was a bit of a plain Jane and was rather shy, particularly camera shy.

Allie never considered a career in modeling because of the skimpy clothing that models had to wear (if the photo shoot required them to wear clothes at all). Then again, few modeling agencies would've hired Allie in the first place. She had the wrong body type—not tall enough, not skinny enough, and her neck was not long enough (though she had the high cheekbones for it).

Cindy finally found a maroon gown that didn't offend her *too* much. "What about this one?" she asked.

"For one thing, it's the wrong color," Allie said.

"Oh, yeah, light green."

After several minutes of arguing and pouring over the racks of clothing, the two friends compromised enough to agree on something. The pastel-green bridesmaid dress was sleeveless, but at least the hemline was below the knee, and the décolletage was kept to a bare minimum.

With the decision made, Tiffany cheerfully suggested to

Cindy, "Now, why don't you try this on while the bride puts on her wedding gown to see if the alterations are going to work?"

Cindy and Allie both agreed, and then Tiffany led them to the dressing rooms. This time Allie's wedding gown fit like a silken glove. She couldn't believe how beautiful she looked in it. When she stepped out of the changing room, she saw Cindy in her bridesmaid's dress. It was still too light on material for either one of their tastes, but Allie had learned to pick her battles carefully.

"Better?" Tiffany asked Allie.

"Now my gown truly *is* perfect!" Allie gushed.

"And you?" Tiffany asked as she turned to Cindy.

"I've never felt so objectified in my entire life," Cindy groused, "but it is Allie's wedding, not mine, so I guess I'll just have to go along with it."

Cindy decided that she wanted to try on more clothes, so Allie patiently waited while Tiffany assisted her. While Allie waited, a tall blonde with a heavily made-up face entered the store and strode confidently toward Allie. A look of recognition passed over the woman's face, and she exclaimed, "Allie McAllister?"

Allie took a closer look at the woman, but she couldn't place her.

"We both went to Barack Obama High School," the woman said.

"I … I'm sorry … I …" Allie stammered as she racked her brain for who the woman might be.

The mystery woman eventually felt she'd kept her former classmate in suspense long enough and said, "My name was Charles Lang back then."

Allie did a double take; she remembered a Charles Lang from Barack Obama High School. He was a couple of grades ahead of her and had been a popular athlete. And now—he had become a woman!

"Even when I was in high school, I realized that all of my macho posturing was only a way to cover up the fact that I was, deep down, a woman trapped in a man's body. So I had the operation done a couple of years ago," the blonde disclosed.

"Oh," Allie replied. She didn't know what else to say; she certainly wasn't going to congratulate him/her for his/her decision.

"Anyway, my name is Charlene now. So are you looking for a wedding dress as well?"

"Yes. Well, actually, I've already found one," Allie answered.

"May I see it?" Charlene asked excitedly.

Allie was still trying to take in the *alteration* in her former classmate, but she politely showed the altered wedding gown.

Just then, Cindy came out of the dressing room, wearing a white tuxedo. "Maybe I should wear *this* instead," she teased.

"Please, Cindy. Jack's family is really conservative, not to mention my own family, and I'm pretty conservative myself, for that matter."

But before Allie could admonish her further, Charlene interrupted. "So you two are getting married? To each other? You know, I always had a feeling about the two of you."

"*What?* No, I'm definitely marrying a man," Allie quickly corrected her.

"Congratulations. So am I," Charlene said.

"I guess I was wrong in my assumption," the former Charles apologized.

"You certainly were," Cindy said. Then she whispered to Allie, "Who *is* this person, anyway?"

"This is Charles … er, I mean *Charlene* Lang, formally

known as Charles Lang. He … er … that is, *she* went to Barack Obama High School with us," Allie stammered.

Cindy looked quizzical "She did?"

"Yes, I played power forward on the boys' basketball team," Charlene said.

"Oh, I get it. Boy, did you have a lot of work done!" Cindy said. "But if it makes you happy, then good for you!"

"Well, it was nice meeting you … or seeing you again … or whatever," a confused Allie babbled as Cindy went to change.

Then the two friends quickly paid for their purchases and left their former classmate alone to be assisted by Tiffany.

Chapter 9

Jack's Back

Allie wanted to photographically document her wedding day for posterity. She found a photographer in the same strip mall where she had found Let Them Eat Cake. The business was named Picture Perfect, and the photographer and proprietor was a tall, lanky man in his forties with sandy blond hair, a moustache of matching hue, and spectacles. He introduced himself as John Denny, and he sat down with Allie to discuss the particulars.

"First of all, so I can get a feel for the scope of the event, are we talking of a happy couple, a thruple, a quad—"

"*Only* a couple," Allie interrupted. "One bride, one groom, and hopefully no waiting."

"Ah, a traditional wedding. I haven't done one of those for quite a long time. And how many bridesmaids and groomsmen will there be?"

"Only two—the maid of honor and the best man," Allie informed him.

"Perhaps I should leave my wide-angle lens at home," Mr. Denny quipped.

After obtaining the photographer, engaging a florist (named Everything Is Coming Up Roses), and renting a social hall in

Darwin City, Allie was nearly finished with all of her wedding preparations. The only problem was that she couldn't find any ministers in all of the Twin Cities who would perform a traditional wedding ceremony. They all seemed to take offense at the very idea of a wife pledging to "submit" herself to her own husband.

As the proposed wedding date drew near, Allie grew concerned that they still didn't have a minister to perform the ceremony; she also was concerned with not having a groom to be wedded to. The fighting in the Middle East was intense, and Allie watched the news reports with increasing alarm. Her betrothed wrote whenever he could, but even though he tried to put on a brave face in his epistles, Allie knew better. There was a frighteningly real possibility that her future husband might soon become past tense.

Allie knew that *absent from the body* meant *present with the Lord,* and she would not begrudge her groom the joy of his glorification. But she would certainly prefer him being present with her for as long as possible. Having waited for years to find her husband, she found the notion cruel that he could be taken away from her so soon before their wedding day; that instead of being united in holy matrimony on earth, she might have to wait decades more to be reunited with him in heaven.

Then Allie heard the glorious news—the war was over! The soldiers were coming back home. In the days that followed, Allie was plagued with the fear that Jack would die in an airplane crash while returning home. But to her relief, the plane arrived, and her betrothed deplaned, and before she knew it, he was walking toward her. Allie ran at top speed and jumped right into Jack's waiting arms.

"You're back," Allie murmured as she cuddled her groom. "Thank God you're back, safe and sound."

"I have returned," Jack confirmed as he kissed his bride's waiting lips.

"Just in the nick of time," Allie reminded him as they walked through the terminal, side by side and hand in hand. "The wedding is weeks away."

"Yes," Jack acknowledged, "and I'm sorry I left you to make all of the wedding arrangements by yourself."

"Uncle Sam has no sense of romance," Allie said with a pout.

"And how are the wedding arrangements coming?" Jack asked.

"Finished, for the most part, except that I can't find a minister who will agree to perform a wedding ceremony where the traditional vows are spoken. They won't even allow the phrase *love, honor, and cherish*, much less the word *obey*. And most of them wanted to substitute *'til death do us part* with *for as long we both love each other* or some such nonsense! Some of them, the woman ministers especially, even objected to my taking your last name."

"A scandalously backward notion," Jack observed, as the two of them exited the airport terminal and made their way to the parking lot where Allie had parked her car.

"I don't care. I am proud to become Mrs. Jack Holtz," Allie stated emphatically. "Besides, it's an easy transition to make. Your last name is much shorter than mine, so it will be easier to write."

"Bravo!" Jack cheered as they reached Allie's automobile. "But I wouldn't worry too much about the minister. I wrote to my pastor back home in Nebraska and asked him to perform the ceremony, and he's agreed."

"You stinker!" Allie exclaimed as she playfully slapped him on the arm. "Why didn't you *tell* me? It would've saved me a whole lot of trouble."

"I'm sorry," Jack said as he got into the passenger seat. "It was supposed to be a surprise—a wedding present, even."

"You and your surprises." Allie sighed in exasperation as she got behind the wheel. "You may be the *only* soldier in history to survive the battlefield, only to be murdered by his intended bride a matter of hours after returning home from the war!"

Allie took her beau to his efficiency apartment so that he could unpack his things. Allie then went back to their new apartment. Besides arranging the details for the wedding, Allie also had been busy finding a place for the newly wedded couple to live. She managed to find a nice one-bedroom apartment in a relatively safe neighborhood in downtown Minneapolis for a reasonable price (no mean feat).

Allie had already moved over most of her belongings from her mother's house to the new apartment and was now sleeping there most nights as well. Later on, as previously agreed upon, Jack drove over to see their new apartment (and to move some of his stuff over too). Allie showed Jack around the place (living room, kitchenette, one bedroom, one bath), and then they ended up in the living room, sitting close together on the couch.

They sat for several minutes, speaking in low voices, holding hands. Inevitably, the soon-to-be wedded couple began to kiss. This was hardly the first time they had kissed, but with absence making the heart grow fonder, and with the pleasure of once again being in each other's company, the kiss became much more passionate than ever before.

Before the situation got any steamier, Jack broke off the kiss and said, "Maybe I should go before we do something we will both regret later."

"But we'll be married in only a few days," Allie argued. "What difference would it make now?"

Jack stood up. "Allie, do we really want to cheat during the last leg of the race, when we are so close to the finish line?"

"I suppose not," Allie said with eyes downcast. Now that the moment was over, she felt ashamed of her behavior.

Jack bent down and pecked Allie's cheek. "Goodbye, Allie. Only a little while longer, and we will truly be together— legally speaking and, more important, according to God's law."

"Goodbye, my love," Allie replied. She stood up and lightly kissed her betrothed's cheek in return. "Thank you for having the strength to resist temptation. Now I *know* I'm marrying the right man."

Jack left Allie in their new place and drove back over to his old one to sleep there alone. Allie went to bed in their new apartment, thankful to God that Jack's cooler head had prevailed in the midst of their precarious situation.

Chapter **10**

Bridal Enthusiasm

The wedding day finally arrived. Allie had spent the previous night at home with her family, as a fond farewell to the place where she had grown up, with the people with whom she had grown up. Cindy had wanted to throw a wild bachelorette party in her friend's honor, but Allie had demurred.

Jack had spent the evening hanging out with his brothers, but the soiree did not involve any alcoholic beverages, strippers, strange women jumping out of cakes, or anything sordid like that.

The next day, minutes before the wedding, Allie was in the antechamber of the small, mainline-denomination church, located in Minneapolis, which she had rented for the occasion. She was getting ready for the ceremony, attended by her mother and her maid of honor.

"I am overjoyed to finally see this day," Billie McAllister enthused as she helped her daughter attach her veil.

"You and me both, Mom," Allie agreed. "I thought I never would see this day come, and I am *so* glad that I can truly wear white on my wedding day."

"But *every* bride wears white on her wedding day," a confused Cindy interjected.

"Yes, but wearing white used to mean that the bride had remained pure until her marriage," Mrs. McAllister explained, "and I, for one, am overflowing with pride that my only daughter has had the resolve to maintain her virginity until this very day."

As her mother hugged her gently, so she wouldn't wrinkle the wedding gown, Allie ruefully remembered that night in the apartment when she had almost given in, and she was once again thankful to God that Jack had possessed the fortitude to say no.

"The importance of maintaining one's purity until marriage was already changing when I was young," Billie continued. Then she honestly confessed to her daughter, "I'm afraid I cannot claim to have been pristine when I married your father."

"But you didn't know any better, Mama," Allie replied softly. "You weren't a Christian back then."

"I don't understand what's so great about purity anyway," Cindy said petulantly. Then she left to join the best man, Jack's elder brother, James, in the church's foyer so they could lock arms and enter the sanctuary together.

Allie gazed at her reflection in the full-length mirror for a while longer. She only had a few moments before her veil would be dropped over her face; then she would gaze upon gauze. Besides her wedding gown and her long, white-lace veil, she wore a pair of white Victorian-style shoes. To complete her look, a local beautician had arranged Allie's hair in ringlets, once referred to as *sausage curls*.

Then mother and daughter left the antechamber together and regally walked to the sanctuary. As she waited for her musical cue, Allie felt a mixture of nervousness and unbridled joy. Eventually, the dulcet strains of Wagner's "Bridal Chorus" came wafting their way, and then the mother of the bride led her daughter past the ushers (Jack's younger brother, Sam, and Allie's older brother, Rod) and down the aisle to the sounds of the oohs and aahs of the gathered—and now standing—throng. They stopped in front of the pastor, and Billie Jo McAllister tearfully gave her only daughter away.

Owing to Allie's giddy enthusiasm, the events of the happiest day of her life flashed before her eyes, much like a series of snapshots. She vaguely heard Pastor Drake recount the instituting of marriage from Genesis 2, and Jesus Christ's application of this passage in Matthew 19, and Paul's delineation of the roles of husband and wife in Ephesians 5. And she could hardly fail to notice as Cindy rolled her eyes at the very mention of a wife submitting to her husband.

But Allie managed to stay focused long enough to recite her vows to take John "Jack" David Holtz, as her "lawfully wedded husband, to have and to hold, from this forward, for better, for worse, for richer, for poorer, in sickness and in health, until death do us part." And she thrilled to hear Jack recite his vows to her. Then there followed the exchanging of the rings, the lighting of the unity candle, and finally, Pastor Drake pronouncing them man and wife—and their first kiss as a married couple.

After skipping down the aisle to the accompaniment of Mendelssohn's "Wedding March," they returned to dismiss the guests, row by row. After posing for a multitude of pictures for the photographer, they exited the church building while being pelted by handfuls of fake rice. Once they got into Jack's automobile (which had been sufficiently covered by nuptial-related graffiti, such as "Just Married" and the like), it was off to the wedding reception.

The Darwin City Social Hall was a rather small edifice, but the wedding guests were slight in number, so an intimate setting was definitely in order. Allie didn't have many friends at school (particularly following her conversion to Christ), and most of Jack's relatives had not bothered to make the trek from Nebraska, other than his immediate family—Mr. and Mrs. David Holtz and their other four sons.

In the spirit of letting bygones be bygones, Allie had invited many of her former classmates and even some of her former instructors, but most of them didn't show. One who did show was Ms. Nye, dressed in a sleeveless black dress that showed off her tattoos, which were currently in vogue, and accompanied by her "wife" of six years.

During the reception, Ms. Nye managed to corner Allie before the blushing bride even had a chance to sit down. "I suppose I shouldn't be surprised," Ms. Nye said, "knowing your backward views, but I simply cannot believe all that drivel regarding submission!"

"But it's easy to submit to a man like Jack, who loves me as Christ loves the church," Allie tried to explain. Her former teacher simply shook her head in disgust, turned on her spiked heels, and walked away from her.

Allie then sat down at the head table. After the speeches were finished, she turned her attention to Pastor Drake (a balding, bespectacled man in his early forties, of average height and build), who was seated at the same table, along with her mother and her brother, the Holtz family, and Ms. Cindy Lake.

"Pastor Drake," Allie said, "how have you remained an active minister and yet avoided having to perform gay weddings? Or *have* you performed gay weddings?"

"A pastor cannot be found guilty of breaking the discrimination laws unless he performs weddings for heterosexual couples only and not for homosexual ones as well. I don't perform weddings at all back in Nebraska—at least not in public."

"But you just performed this wedding in public," Allie pointed out.

"Yes, but by coming to Minnesota for the wedding and leaving soon afterward, I hope to fly under the radar of the local government, so to speak."

At the reception, after cutting the cake and much feasting and dancing—and in the newlywed couple's case, much kissing—Cindy came up to Allie and said, "I can't *believe* that your husband's pastor still believes in that fairy tale of Adam and Eve! Everyone knows that we evolved from apes."

"I haven't believed that since before I was a teenager," Allie countered.

"Yeah, I remember your creative exam answers in Ms. Nye's biology class. Unlike your outmoded doctrine, though my belief in reincarnation totally agrees with the tenets of evolution. It's all a process from amoebas, to apes, to humans, to God!"

"That's not what the Holy Bible teaches," Allie argued.

"Oh, that's your standard answer for everything," Cindy retorted.

The newlyweds left the reception soon after to embark on their happy honeymoon. As Jack drove his greatly chivalried car away, he asked his new wife, "So did your wedding day live up to your cherished dreams?"

Allie kissed her new husband on the cheek and excitedly replied, "It exceeded even my wildest dreams! You've made me feel like the most blessed woman in the whole wide world!"

Chapter 11

Pregnant Pause

After honeymooning for a week at a hotel adjacent to the Mall of America in Bloomington, Minnesota (they could hardly have afforded to go to Paris or even to Niagara Falls), the newlyweds settled down in domestic tranquility in their new apartment. For now, Allie still worked her waitressing job at the Gopher Diner, and she enrolled in classes at Edina Community College for her upcoming junior year. Jack was also enrolled at ECC for his junior year, and he continued to serve in the Army Reserve.

But early during the first semester of her junior year, Allie began to experience bouts of nausea in the morning. She could certainly make an educated guess as to the cause, but she made an appointment with her family physician. Allie's doctor was a bright, young physician, just out residency, named Dr. Laura Ward.

Dr. Ward was a tall, rather attractive woman in her late twenties, with light-brown hair and big brown eyes. Dr. Ward ran a series of tests on Allie, and after a time, she returned to the examining room to discuss the results.

Allie waited impatiently as she sat on the rather uncomfortable examining table.

Dr. Ward informed Allie, "The results came back as positive."

"Positive," Allie repeated. "Does that mean that it's good news?"

"I suppose that all depends on whether or not you wanted to get pregnant."

"Well, I did want to get pregnant," Allie admitted, "just not this soon."

Her physician mildly scolded her. "Now, Allie, you really should know better than to stop taking your birth control pills at your age."

"I've never taken the pill. I've never had any reason to. I waited until I was married to engage in any activity that could cause me to get pregnant."

"Then you should have started taking birth control pills after you got married. You're much too young to be having a child."

"Are you saying that my life may be in danger if I have this baby?"

"Not necessarily. I was talking more about your quality of life. Do you really want to be saddled with a child when you're only twenty or twenty-one?"

"Other mothers have had children much younger than that."

"In times past they have, but not in this day and age. At any rate, I would be derelict in my duties as a physician if I did not advise you to have an abortion."

"Have an abortion simply because a child may impinge upon my quality of life?" Allie railed. "I wouldn't have an abortion if my life literally depended upon it!"

"All right, Allie. I cannot force you to have an abortion, not under the current laws at any rate. But in my professional opinion, you are making a huge mistake."

"Children are a gift from God," Allie countered, "so how can this possibly be a mistake?"

Dr. Ward sighed. "Since you are resolved to go through with it, I will recommend a good ob-gyn and a quality hospital for you to receive your 'gift.'"

"Could you recommend any that offer free delivery?" Allie quipped.

Allie may have sounded resolved, but inwardly, she was concerned. Dr. Ward was right about one thing: bringing a child to full term sounded like a daunting, even potentially dangerous task. Allie also was not looking forward to the other aspects of her pregnancy—morning sickness, weight gain, retaining water. And the idea of enduring the labor pains scared her half to death!

But Allie also knew that she would never agree to have an abortion. Ending an innocent child's life for the sake of convenience or even to save her own life was anathema to her. Besides, as she had just told her doctor, she really did want children someday—just not so soon after her wedding day.

Allie drove home and found her husband sitting on the living room sofa.

"I'm pregnant," she informed him plainly.

"Are you sure?" Jack asked.

"The doctor is sure. You don't sound overjoyed with the news."

"Of course I'm overjoyed. It's only that this is so unexpected."

"Accidents will happen." Allie tried to bring some levity into the situation.

"But this accident means one more mouth to feed, and one less income to pay for it," Jack observed much more seriously.

"So? God will take care of us. Next I suppose you're going to advise me to have an abortion, like my doctor just did!" Allie answered peevishly.

Jack got up off of the couch to put his arms around his upset wife. He kissed her tenderly on her right cheek. "Of course I'm not going to tell you to get an abortion! I'm sorry for my initial reaction, Allie. It just caught me off guard. You're right; God *will* take care of us. I'll get a second job if I have to."

"Thank you," Allie murmured as she cuddled closer to her hubby. "I just couldn't handle this situation if I didn't have your support."

"You'll always have my love and support," Jack promised her.

Allie let Jack tell his family the joyous news, and she dutifully called her own mother and announced, "Mom, I have some news. I'm pregnant!"

"That's wonderful news! I wasn't expecting to become a grandmother quite so soon, but I couldn't be happier."

"I wasn't expecting to be expecting so soon either," Allie replied, relieved that her mother was taking the news better than her husband had.

Next, Allie called Cindy.

"Hey, Al Pal, what's new?" Cindy asked after she'd answered the phone.

"For one thing, I'm pregnant!" Allie announced.

"Oh, Allie. What happened? You forget to take your birth control pills?"

"I don't take the pill," Allie reminded her feminist friend.

"Well, no wonder you got pregnant then!"

"I wanted to get pregnant—or at least I wanted to get pregnant eventually."

"Eventually is right. You're way too young to have a child."

"So twenty years old is too young to get married and to have a child?" Allie asked.

"Well, duh!" Cindy responded. "How will you ever embark on a fulfilling career when you're saddled with children?"

"I don't *want* a 'fulfilling career'; I only want to be a wife and a mother."

"What backward notions you have, Allie Cat."

"That's what the Bible instructs women to do—'Teach the young women to be sober, to love their husbands, to love their children, to be discreet, chaste, keepers at home, good, obedient to their own husbands, that the word of God be not blasphemed,'" Allie said, quoting Titus 2:4–5.

"Don't be ridiculous, Allie Cat. No sane woman wants to live like that anymore!"

"I do," Allie pointed out.

"You're a better woman than I am, Allie McAllister."

"Thank you, but the name is Allie Holtz now."

"Okay, Mrs. Holtz, but you have your whole life ahead of you. Why do you want to ruin it by becoming a mother? Besides that, you've only recently gotten married. Shouldn't you enjoy married life with your new husband before you burden yourself with children?"

"That was the original plan, but I guess that God had other ideas. Besides, I've wanted children for almost as long as I've wanted a husband. Children aren't a burden; they are a 'heritage of the Lord.'"

"You're a nut, Al Pal."

CHAPTER 12

A Maid of Honor Dishonored

It was about a week later when Allie received a phone call one morning.

"Is this Ms. Allie McAllister?"

"Actually, I'm Mrs. Allie Holtz now," Allie corrected, "but yes, this is she."

"And do you know a Ms. Cynthia Lake?" the voice asked.

Suspicious, Allie asked, "Who wants to know?"

"I'm calling from Richard Dawkins Memorial Hospital in Minneapolis. Ms. Lake listed you as the person to contact in the case of an emergency—"

"There's been an *emergency*?" Allie exclaimed. "What happened?"

"There was an incident involving Ms. Lake on campus," the speaker answered, somewhat evasively.

Cindy Lake was enrolled at a major university located in Minneapolis. Unlike her good friend Allie, Cindy had no trouble gaining admittance to the college because she wholeheartedly adhered to all of the dictates of a progressive, postmodern education.

"I'll be right there," Allie promised the caller.

Jack was working, so Allie grabbed her car keys and drove

down to the hospital herself. When Allie eventually found Cindy's hospital room, she entered it and found her friend lying in bed, curled up in fetal position, weeping profusely.

Allie gasped. "What happened to you, Cin?"

"There w-was this guy," Cindy tried to explain through her sobs, "who lived on the same floor as me in the dorm. The s-star quarterback on the f-football team, and he said he wanted t-to t-talk." Here, Cindy burst into tears.

Allie sat down in a nearby chair, leaned close, and put her arms around her distraught friend.

After composing herself somewhat, Cindy tried again. "So I invited him into my d-dorm room and—"

"Cindy! How *could* you?" Allie admonished her.

"I thought that he was cute. Cute guys usually don't pay any attention to me. Anyway, we started out talking, and then he began to kiss me. And then ..." Here Cindy broke down again.

Allie gave her friend time to collect herself once more before she probed further. "Were you ... raped?"

Cindy simply let out a mighty wail. Once she had again composed herself, she whimpered, "Why did he have to do that to me? I would have given myself to him fully when the time was right."

"That is *not* what the act of sex is for," Allie said.

"Sex should only be by mutual consent," Cindy said, dutifully repeating what she had been taught in school.

"I don't mean only that," Allie countered. "Of course, sex should only be performed by consenting adults. But the real reason for sexual intercourse is to show mutual love and respect between a husband and a wife. And for procreation, of course."

Cindy forced a wan smile. "There you go with those crazy ideas of yours. Though maybe if I'd listened to some of those crazy ideas, I wouldn't have ended up here."

Allie simply held her best friend's hand. Obviously, she wasn't about to say *I told you so* at that particular moment.

Then Cindy sighed. "I certainly don't feel loved or respected after that experience." The two friends sat in silence for a while. Then Cindy asked, "It's not like that between Jack and you, is it?"

"No, Jack and I love each other very much," Allie answered softly.

"I envy you, Allie. For the first time in my life, I envy you."

Cindy convalesced in the hospital for a few days, and Allie visited her greatly traumatized friend daily. When it came time for Cindy's discharge, Allie asked her, "What are you going to do now?"

"I guess I'll wait to see if I'm pregnant. If I am, then I'll have to get an abortion."

"That would be like making a bad situation even worse," Allie contended.

"I have the right to choose what I do with my own body."

"Then you should have exercised that right before you invited that guy into your dorm room in the first place," Allie pointed out.

"Look, I don't want to argue about the 'sanctity of life' issue right now!"

"All right, Cindy, no more arguing, but you're not thinking of going back to the coed dorms after this, are you?"

"To tell you the truth," Cindy answered, "I'm rather afraid to do so now."

Allie simply nodded her understanding. "And your mother is still MIA?"

"As far as I know, she's still traveling in Europe," Cindy answered.

Cindy had mostly been raised by her grandparents, who were now both deceased. Cindy's mother, Vivian Lake, was always more like an older sister, one who would drop by from time to time to see her offspring. A few years after giving birth to her only child and having shed the weight gained while pregnant, Vivian became a famous fashion model. Cindy hadn't seen or heard from her mother since she was sixteen years old; she never knew her father.

"Jack and I have discussed it, and we think you should move in with us, at least until you get back on your feet, emotionally speaking," Allie offered.

"Really?" Cindy's face brightened "That's awfully kind of you, Allie."

"You're my best friend, Cindy. Besides, it's not that magnanimous of an offer. All we can provide for you is a couch to sleep on."

"Still, it's better than a park bench," Cindy acknowledged. "I'll take it."

Cindy moved in with Allie and Jack, and living with Cindy was a whole new experience for the newlyweds. Cindy constantly criticized Jack for subjugating his wife to a life of virtual slavery as a wife and prospective mother.

Jack implied that Cindy should earn her keep by helping Allie with the household chores (an affront to Cindy's feminist sensibilities).

One day, Cindy groused to her best friend, "What's with that male chauvinist pig of a husband of yours, laying down the law and telling me how to live my life?"

"You know, Cin, you *are* a houseguest here," Allie gently reminded her.

Cindy eventually submitted to the house rules, even if she didn't like them or understand them. Cindy had dropped out of college—at least for the remainder of the first semester of her senior year—so Cindy and Allie spent a lot of time together, much more time than Allie spent with her own husband. Jack was either at work (he was now employed as a security guard) or in class, and the resulting separation was hard on the newlywed couple.

But whenever he was home, Jack was totally attentive to his new wife. Despite how dead tired he was, he still insisted on waiting on the mother-to-be, hand and foot, even though Cindy was now well enough to earn her keep by doing the cooking, cleaning, and the laundry (which she reluctantly did whenever Jack was away). Thus, Cindy witnessed firsthand how a self-sacrificing Christian husband loved his wife as Christ loved the church and how a loving couple treated one another.

This was something that Cindy had never before observed. Cindy's mother had decided at the age of eighteen that she wanted a child, and so she stopped taking the pill. However, Vivian Lake also decided that she did not want a husband. Cindy's biological father did not relish the responsibility of marriage and fatherhood, so he complied and left her alone. Vivian soon enough tired of the joys of motherhood. Cindy was raised by her grandparents (though in actual fact, she was raised by a succession of day-care centers).

CHAPTER **13**

From Perversion to Conversion

The somewhat harmonious life between the three apartment mates was soon enough disturbed when Jack received orders to report for temporary duty at Fort Hood, located in Killeen, Texas.

"Not again!" Allie exclaimed when her husband relayed the bad news to her. "And so near to Autumn Festival weekend?" (Autumn Festival was the progressive, postmodern equivalent of Thanksgiving.)

"When Uncle Sam calls the tune, you have to dance where he tells you to."

"Uncle Sam has *no* holiday spirit," Allie groaned.

But no matter how unhappy both of them were with the news, Jack left for the assignment as ordered. Allie stayed behind and continued to prepare for the birth of their first child. Due to her difficult pregnancy, Allie's doctor had advised her to take it easy. She wasn't bedridden, but she had to quit her job, and of course, she had already "packed in" college. So Mrs. Holtz was thankful that she had Miss Lake to keep her company.

One night, Allie was sitting in bed, doing one of her "strange religious rituals" (as Cindy called it), praying and

67

reading her Bible, when she was interrupted by a gentle rapping on her bedroom door.

"What do I have to do?" Cindy asked after she entered the bedroom.

"I-I'm sorry," Allie stammered. "Do you mean what chores do you have to do tomorrow?"

"No, I mean, what do I have to do to get what *you* got—the peace, the joy, the forgiveness, and the love that you and Jack have for each other and for other people, like me."

Allie hadn't done a lot of witnessing in her life, mostly because most people wrote her off as a religious kook long before she could explain why she had hope within her. But she had tried to witness to Cindy over the years, so Allie gathered her thoughts and once again explained to her friend. "You have to admit to God that you're a sinner and to repent of your sins. And you have to believe that Jesus Christ's death on the cross is the only way to pay for those sins. And you need to accept Jesus Christ as your personal Lord and Savior."

Cindy had no problem believing that she was a sinner, given her issues with pride. She prayed and accepted Jesus Christ as her Lord and Savior that very night.

Allie knew that Cindy's conversion was genuine, particularly when she perceived positive changes in her best friend right away. Cindy immediately became more sober-minded (and just plain sober, period), less selfish, and more cheerfully helpful around the apartment. When Jack returned from his TDY (just in time for Christmas), Cindy asked Allie not to tell him of her recent conversion; she wanted to see if Jack noticed the improvements.

On his first day back, Jack saw a difference in their temporary lodger, particularly in her personality—her less-complaining spirit, the absence of her usual mocking tone, the lack of her feminist tirades. The next morning, when the young married couple sat down at the kitchen table for their morning devotions, and Cindy joined them with her borrowed Bible in hand, the jig was definitely up.

"Something tells me that we are not dealing with the same old sinful Cynthia Lake," Jack observed.

"No, you're not," Cindy confirmed with a Cheshire cat smile. "I've changed. Or rather, I'm being changed—every day."

"Being conformed to the image of Christ," Allie supplied.

"Praise the Lord!" Jack exulted. "Will wonders never cease?"

After celebrating a wonderful Christmas morning together, Cindy informed her roommates, "I've come to a decision. I'm going back to college."

"Not back to the coed dorms?" Allie asked, worried.

"No, of course not," Cindy assured her. "I'm going to resume classes next semester, but I won't be living on campus ever again. I've already secured an apartment near the university."

"You're welcome to stay here if you'd like," Jack offered. "You would be a great help to Allie if ever I'm deployed again."

"I appreciate that," Cindy said, "and I thank God for everything that you two have done for me. But I feel it's time for me to leave the nest and spread my wings and fly. Don't worry, though; if ever Allie needs me, I'll be there."

The Holtzes were sorry to see Cindy go, but they wished her well and promised to pray for her daily. As Cindy settled into her new apartment, Jack resettled into his. The married couple was ecstatic to be reunited. On Cupid's Day, Jack brought home a large, brightly decorated chocolate cake (bought at Let Them Eat Cake) and a long faux-pearl necklace in honor of the second anniversary of their first date. As Jack was clasping the necklace around his wife's lovely neck, the phone rang. Allie answered and heard, "Happy Cupid's Day, Allie Cat!"

"Cindy!" Allie said. "So how's college life?"

"It's okay. But thanks to you converting me, I'm no longer the ideal student that I used to be. I argue far too much with the professors now—just like your hubby."

"Blame it on the Holy Spirit," Allie said.

"But enough about me. How was your Cupid's Day? What did you get?"

"So far it's been wonderful. Jack bought me a beautiful fake-pearl necklace and a beautiful *real* chocolate cake with chocolate frosting."

"You'd better take it easy on the cake," Cindy warned her. "You're gonna gain enough weight with your pregnancy."

"Don't remind me. How are things otherwise?" Allie asked.

"Well, as you know, I had to quit my receptionist job at the abortion clinic, so money's been a little tight lately."

"I'm glad to hear that you're sticking to your guns," Allie said, "but I'm sorry to hear about the loss of income."

"Don't be. My relationship with Jesus Christ is far more important to me than earning filthy lucre. I guess that I'll just have to find more honest work."

"I hear that the Gopher Diner has an opening," Allie said mischievously.

"I'm not that much of a masochist, but hey, I haven't told you the best news yet. I've tracked down my mother!"

"That's great news!"

"Yep. She's coming back to Minneapolis for a visit. I can't wait to tell her about my new faith!" Cindy exclaimed.

A couple of weeks after Cupid's Day, there was a loud knock upon the Holtzes' apartment door. Since Jack was at work, Allie opened the door and found herself face-to-face with two uniformed police officers.

"Ms. Allie McAllister?" one of the officers inquired.

"Actually, it's Mrs. Allie Holtz now," she corrected him.

"Mrs. Holtz, could you come down to the station and answer some questions regarding a Ms. Cynthia Lake?" the second officer (a woman) asked. It was clear from her tone that Allie's obedience was compulsory.

Chapter 14

Arrested Development

Allie was somewhat worried by the officer's request, but then she simply figured that Cindy had decided to press rape charges. Allie got into the police cruiser and was driven down to the police station. Once there, the officers took her to an interrogation room. Again, she felt uneasy, but the officers had said she was wanted for questioning, not that she was under arrest. After a short interval, Allie was joined by a large, fortysomething woman with long, wavy ash-blonde hair. She identified herself as Detective Melissa Smith.

"You are Ms. Allison Jane McAllister?" Detective Smith asked.

"Yes," Allie answered, "only now it's Mrs. Allison Jane Holtz."

"Sorry, Mrs. Holtz," the detective said. "Pardon me, but who takes her husband's name in this day and age?" She shook her head and then said, "And you are familiar with a Ms. Cynthia Ann Lake?"

"Yes. Cindy and I have been best friends since middle school."

"And Ms. Lake was your houseguest last autumn?"

"Yes, she was, Detective Smith."

"And during that time, did she exhibit any unusual behavior?"

"Well," Allie pondered, "she was understandably shaken up after her rape."

"And what about several weeks following her rape? Did her behavior strike you as odd in any way?"

"What do you mean?"

"We have reports of her suddenly acting differently than she ever had acted—abruptly quitting her job at the local Planned Population Control abortion clinic, practicing celibacy, even reading the Bible, of all things—"

"Oh! If that's what you mean by unusual behavior, then yes, she did act that way while she was staying with us," Allie admitted.

"Do you have any idea why Ms. Lake started acting contrary to her usual behavior?"

Of course, Allie was fully aware of why Cindy had changed her ways, but she was also fully aware of the state's laws regarding proselytizing.

"It sounds like she ... became a Christian."

"Yes, and do you know how she became a Christian, Mrs. Holtz?" Detective Smith's tone indicated she already knew the answer.

At this moment, Allie realized that she should lawyer up, but she remembered Jesus Christ's statement: "For whosoever shall be ashamed of me and my words, of him shall the Son of man be ashamed, when he shall come in his own glory," and she just couldn't bring herself to deny her Lord. So she answered truthfully. "Cindy became a Christian because I led her to the Lord."

"Allison Jane Holtz, I am placing you under arrest for the crime of proselytizing the Christian faith. You have the right to remain silent. If you choose to waive this right, anything that you say can and will be used against you in a court of law. You have the right to an attorney. If you cannot afford an attorney, one will be provided for you."

Allie was handcuffed and led away; then she was fingerprinted, and her mug shot was taken. She was strip-searched and then she was given prison garb. Finally, she was placed in a holding cell. Allie couldn't believe that she was being treated like a common criminal, simply because she had shared her faith. She also couldn't fathom why the law seemed to care more about catching innocent Christians like her than in arresting that depraved rapist who had physically violated her best friend, Cindy.

Allie sat in the holding cell for several minutes, all the while being eyed by her burly cellmates. She finally was granted her phone call, and she called her husband. When he answered, Allie's voice quavered when she said, "J-Jack?"

"Allie? What's wrong?"

"I've been arrested!" Allie dramatically announced.

"Arrested?" Jack repeated in disbelief. "What in God's name for?"

"It *was* in God's name. I've been arrested for proselytizing!"

"I'll get you a good lawyer. In the meantime, keep your mind on things above."

"I'll try to."

"And remember that I love you, and so does Jesus."

"I love you too. Pray for me! And tell my family what's happened."

"I will, and I am praying for you already."

Good lawyers cost money that the Holtzes didn't have, so they had to make do with a court-appointed public defender. Mr. Lloyd Jones met with Allie in the county jail, where she had now been placed, to discuss the particulars of the case. Mr. Jones was a short, stocky man with a balding pate. He arrived wearing a rumpled gray suit.

"Hello, Ms. McAllister, my name is Lloyd Jones. I've been appointed to represent you in court."

Allie shook his proffered hand. "Thank you, Mr. Jones, but the name is Mrs. Holtz."

"Ah, yes. Let's see now. You have been accused of proselytizing?"

"Yes."

"Were there any witnesses to this act?" Mr. Jones asked.

"Only Cindy."

"Ms. Cynthia Ann Lake, the person you are accused of proselytizing?"

"Yes." Then Allie apprehensively asked, "Was she the one who filed the police report against me?"

"No, actually, it was"—Mr. Jones referred to his paperwork—"a Ms. Vivian Lake."

Allie gasped. "Cindy's mother turned me in?"

"That is correct," Mr. Jones confirmed.

"But she hasn't had anything to do with her daughter since Cindy was sixteen years old!"

"It appears she's taken quite an interest in her daughter as of late," Mr. Jones wryly observed.

"Apparently so."

"Now let's talk damage control," Mr. Jones suggested. "According to the police report, you actually admitted your guilt."

"Yes, I did."

"That may make a not-guilty plea rather difficult."

"But I *am* guilty," Allie freely admitted, "and I'd happily share my faith again if it would bring peace to another poor soul who is suffering as much as Cindy was."

"Hmm … considering your religious fervor, we may be able to enter a not-guilty-by-reason-of-insanity plea."

"I am *not* crazy!" Allie cried. "I'm simply a Christian!"

"If the Mental Health Association had their way, there would not be any distinction between those two states of being."

"I bet you that I could've gotten away with telling Cindy about the benefits of yoga or meditation," Allie grumbled.

"Of course. There are no current laws against doing *that.*"

Chapter 15

Lawyered Up

Allie was not impressed with her court-appointed lawyer, but Mr. Jones managed to do one thing for his reluctant client; he was able to lower Allie's bail. Several aspects were taken into consideration in the decision: Mrs. Holtz was not a violent criminal; it was her first offense; and given the Holtzes' dire financial circumstances and that the accused was in her second trimester of pregnancy, she was not considered a flight risk.

Once Allie was breathing the free air again, she met with her family to discuss her next move. They knew that they would prefer a defense attorney who was more sympathetic to their Christian beliefs, but could they even find such a lawyer, particularly in Minnesota? Pastor Drake recommended a lawyer, Brian Volk, from Nebraska, who specialized in these sorts of cases, and the Holtzes contacted him for legal representation.

The East and West Coasts were at the forefront of intolerance toward Christians, but some of the Midwest and the Southern states (the Bible Belt) lagged behind in their progressivism. Owing to an obscure Minnesota law that allowed an accused person to engage an attorney from the state of his or her choice, the Holtzes were able to secure the services of Lawyer Volk, who magnanimously waived his usual fee in deference to the Holtzes' finances.

Mr. Volk met with the Holtzes at the McAllister house to discuss the plan of action. Mr. Volk was a short, intellectual-looking man with short-cropped dark-brown hair, wire-rimmed glasses, and a goatee that gave him a vaguely Mephistophelian air. Mr. Volk spoke quickly and passionately about both Allie's legal situation and his own faith. The gathered group was heartened by his obvious passion and his dedication to Christian principles and also by his assurances that Allie's case was winnable.

"The proselytizing law is a clear violation of the First Amendment of our nation's Constitution: 'Congress shall make no law respecting an establishment of religion, or prohibiting the free exercise thereof,'" Mr. Volk quoted.

"It sure beats copping to an insanity plea," Allie said.

"And challenging the state law may be the only legal avenue left to us," Mr. Volk said, "other than the insanity plea because you've already freely admitted your guilt."

"Oh, how I wish you had never done such a foolish thing!" Mrs. McAllister moaned.

"Would you rather that I'd denied my faith?" Allie asked, though not angrily; she knew that her mother was only worried about her welfare.

"No, I suppose not," Mrs. McAllister admitted quietly.

"I have never been prouder of my little sister," Rod McAllister said. Rod was now twenty-four years old and had grown in his Christian faith and in his boldness in sharing that faith.

"Thank you, Rod," Allie said humbly, "and thank you for referring to me as *little*. It's nice to still be called little, even after all the weight that I've gained with this pregnancy."

"I am also very proud of my wife," Jack said. He was sitting next to Allie on the love seat in the living room, and now he took Allie into his loving arms and kissed her. "Sometimes you just have to take a stand: 'We ought to obey God rather than men.' That's Acts 5:29."

"Get a room, you two," Rod joked.

Jack turned to the lawyer and said, "But I don't understand why *I* haven't been indicted."

"Because it was your wife, specifically, who led Miss Lake to the Lord," Mr. Volk answered.

"I would gladly take her place, if I could," Jack said.

"I would not wish that," Allie replied tenderly.

Just then, there was a tentative knock on the door. Rod opened it to the small, slender figure of Miss Cindy Lake.

"I don't know if I'm even welcome here anymore," Cindy said hesitantly.

"Come on in, Cindy," Mrs. McAllister said warmly. "Of course you're welcome here."

Cindy made a beeline to the love seat and got down on her knees before Allie. "Please forgive me for all of the trouble I've caused you."

"Don't be silly, Cindy," Allie said. "I don't blame you for your mother's actions. No one here blames you for that."

"I had no idea she would do something like this. I simply wanted to tell her what God has done for me," Cindy confessed.

"It's better that I end up in jail than you ending up in hell," Allie replied cheerfully. "Now get up off your knees already. Grab a chair, and sit down."

Cindy grabbed the only chair available, one of the hard, wooden kitchen chairs.

"Cindy, this is Allison's lawyer, Mr. Brian Volk," Mrs. McAllister said. "Mr. Volk, this is Miss Cynthia Ann Lake."

"Ah, Miss Lake." Brian offered her his hand. "I know you by reputation only."

"By bad reputation only," Cindy said as she shook his hand. "Pleased to meet you, Mr. Volk."

"I am also very pleased to meet you," Mr. Volk said. "May I deduce from your words and actions that you are on our side in this case?"

"Yes, I am," Cindy answered, "because you are surely on the Lord's side."

"Good. Then may I rely on you to testify on your best friend's behalf?"

"It is the very least I can do to make amends," Cindy answered contritely.

In the weeks that followed, as they prepared for the trial, they learned more about their adversary. The prosecutor in the case was the assistant district attorney for Hennepin County, Cherie Williams. Ms. Williams was a tall woman in her forties with long dark-brown hair and brown eyes. Ms. Williams made no secret of her attitude toward Christian malefactors like Allison Holtz. She considered it her sworn duty to weed out such subversive individuals for the good of society.

As if to underscore this point, Ms. Williams had added to the existing charge of proselytizing an indictment of criminal political incorrectness. Both of these charges were serious accusations in Minnesota jurisprudence, punishable by a hefty fine and/or a prison sentence of five to ten years. And Ms. Williams had already made it quite clear via the media that she intended to prosecute the defendant to the fullest extent of the law.

The wild card in this scenario was the judge assigned to the case. The Honorable Gloria Dawson was in her mid-forties, with short strawberry-blonde hair. Unlike Ms. Williams's career-woman mode of dress and deportment, Ms. Dawson gave off a slightly more maternal air. The judge was, in fact, a mother and had been legally wed to a man, a rarity in that day and age. She was also a grandmother, although decidedly not grandmotherly in appearance.

Judge Dawson's past record of judicial verdicts and sentencing indicated that she could rule either way in this particular case, as she had previously displayed no bias for or against religious rights. And Judge Dawson's opinion was the one that counted the most in the long run. While jury trials were still held in the state of Minnesota, the sentence would ultimately be decided by the presiding judge.

CHAPTER 16

The State of Minnesota
v. Allison Holtz

It was once said that the wheels of justice turn slowly, but in postmodern, progressive America, they turned with surprising alacrity. Allie's trial started in late April, a scant two months after her arrest. The prosecution thought it was such an open-and-shut case that they needed very little preparation time. So Allie arrived at the courthouse with her lawyer, her loving husband, her cheering committee of family and (her only) friend, and most important, her Lord.

Allie also arrived over seven months pregnant, and she worried about the effect that this activity—not to mention the mental anguish—might have on her pregnancy. Lawyer Volk had filed a motion for postponement of the trial until after Allie gave birth, but the request was denied. So Allie had to waddle into the courtroom on the appointed trial date. Thanks to having posted bail, however, she was allowed to waddle in dressed in a baby-blue maternity dress instead of an orange jumpsuit and manacles.

The courtroom was packed. The Minnesota judicial system had done away with much that had been before, but trials were still open to the public, including the liberal-biased news media. The bailiff announced the entrance of Judge Dawson, and the courtroom rose in response, including Allie, with much difficulty. The State of Minnesota v. Allison Holtz trial was now underway. When Judge Dawson asked how the defendant pled, Allie dutifully answered, as instructed by her lawyer, "Not guilty, Your Honor."

Next were the opening statements. The prosecution led.

"Your Honor, what we have before us is such an open-and-shut case that I am amazed we even have to waste the taxpayers' money on a trial. The defendant, Ms. Allison Holtz, has already admitted her guilt. The state will prove, however, beyond a shadow of a doubt, that Ms. Holtz's proselytizing outside of the confines of a church building—in direct violation of the laws of this state—is only the latest example of her lifelong, flagrant disregard for everything that is good and proper. Thank you."

At least they finally got my last name right, Allie thought, *even if they still persist in referring to me as Ms. instead of Mrs.*

Then Mr. Volk stood up and addressed the court. "Your Honor, the defense will prove that not only is my client, Mrs. Allison Jane Holtz, a law-abiding citizen, provided that the laws of the land do not interfere with the free exercise of her religion, but that she is, in fact, not guilty of any offense whatsoever, as this proselytizing law is, in itself, unconstitutional! Thank you, Your Honor."

Mr. Volk's shocking statement elicited such a commotion in the courtroom that Judge Dawson had to gavel the spectators into silence.

The prosecution presented its case the next day. Assistant District Attorney Williams began by calling Detective Melissa

Smith to the stand. Detective Smith relayed the particulars of her interview with Ms. Holtz. As she spoke, the police report was passed around the jury for inspection.

Before Detective Smith stepped down, Lawyer Volk exercised his right to cross-examine the witness, and he asked her point-blank, "Detective Smith, is it standard practice for the Minneapolis Police Department to interrogate people before they are read their rights?"

ADA Williams was about to object, but her witness beat her to it.

"It was not an interrogation. Your client was only brought in for questioning," Detective Smith answered curtly. "I cannot be blamed if the perp volunteered the information before she had the good sense to lawyer up."

ADA Williams then called various former teachers of Allie's from middle school, high school, and college, like Ms. Nye and Allison's high school history teacher, Mr. Richard, to testify to Allie's politically incorrect views.

During Ms. Nye's testimony regarding Allie's creative exam answers, Mr. Volk said, "Objection, Your Honor. Relevancy."

"Your Honor, I am trying to establish that the accused's disregard for the law is a lifelong condition," Ms. Williams explained.

"Overruled. The witness may continue," Judge Dawson said.

Having lost that round, Mr. Volk refrained from any more objections to these witnesses; it was a fruitless exercise anyway. By the fourth such witness, Professor Kirk, Mr. Volk stood up. "Your Honor, the defense concedes that Mrs. Holtz's Christian beliefs are of long standing."

"I concur. Let's move it along, Madam Prosecutor," Judge Dawson suggested.

"Very well, Your Honor," she agreed. "I will move on to my next witness. The State calls Ms. Charlene Lang."

As Ms. Lang strode to the witness stand in her usual confident manner, Allie wondered just what "Charlene" had to say against her; after all, she hadn't had many dealings with Charles Lang, and she had only met Charlene Lang once since high school.

As soon as Ms. Lang was sworn in, ADA Williams said, "Ms. Lang, would you please tell this court, in your own words, what occurred between you and the accused last year?"

"Yes, Ms. Williams," she answered obediently. "I ran into Ms. Holtz at a dress shop called It's Only Fitting. I know her because we went to Barack Obama High School together. During my conversation with her, she referred to me by the *wrong* pronoun."

"Could you please be more specific?" the attorney coached.

"Objection!" Mr. Volk said. "Counsel is leading the witness."

"Overruled," Judge Dawson said. "The witness will please answer the question."

"She referred to me as *he* rather than *she*," Ms. Lang said.

The spectators immediately gasped and then began to murmur among themselves, until Judge Dawson's gavel silenced the room.

Fine. Everybody's shocked that I accidentally referred to someone by the wrong gender pronoun, Allie thought, *but it's okay for them to continually refer to me as Ms. instead of Mrs.*

"And how did this make you feel?" ADA Williams prompted.

"Objection!" Mr. Volk called out again. "Counsel is *definitely* leading the witness this time!"

"Sustained," Judge Dawson agreed. "The witness will refrain from answering the question."

"Please continue with your account, Ms. Lang," the prosecutor requested.

"Naturally, I was quite offended when Allie did that—"

"Objection!" Mr. Volk exclaimed.

"Ms. Williams, pray instruct your witness to *not* disobey my direct instructions, under threat of being held in contempt of court!" Judge Dawson ordered.

"Yes, Your Honor," Ms. Williams said. "No further questions, Your Honor."

"Your witness, Counselor," Judge Dawson instructed.

"Thank you, Your Honor," Counselor Volk acknowledged, and then he turned his attention toward the witness. "*Ms. Lang,*" Brian said pointedly, making no attempt to hide his sarcasm, "isn't it true that back when you and Allie were in high school together, you were actually a male?"

"Objection!" Ms. Williams interrupted. "If Ms. Lang self-identifies as a female, then she has always *been* a female."

"Sustained," Judge Dawson ruled. "The witness will disregard the question."

"But isn't it true, Ms. Lang," Attorney Volk said, "that since the last time my client saw you in high school, you've had a sex-change operation and plastic surgery and that you take hormones in order to fully realize the female that you have always been?"

"Objection!"

"On what grounds?" the judge asked the ADA.

Ms. Williams fumbled. "I … withdraw the objection, Your Honor."

"The witness will answer the question," Judge Dawson said.

"Yes, I have had all that work done to reveal my *true* self," Charlene admitted.

"Ms. Lang, do you think that Mrs. Holtz was purposely attempting to demean you?" Mr. Volk asked.

"Objection. Calls for speculation on the part of the witness," Ms. Williams said.

"Objection sustained," Judge Dawson ruled.

Mr. Volk tried again. "Did you get the impression that Mrs. Holtz meant it in a malicious way?"

"Objection. Same reason," ADA Williams said.

"Overruled," Judge Dawson decided. "I'm going to allow the question this time."

"No, I suppose Allie only misspoke," Charlene admitted quietly.

"And she immediately corrected herself, did she not?" Mr. Volk asked.

"Yes, she did," Ms. Lang answered sheepishly.

"No further questions, Your Honor," Mr. Volk concluded.

"Would the prosecution like to redirect?" Judge Dawson asked.

"No, Your Honor," the prosecutor said.

"The witness may step down," Judge Dawson said. "Court is adjourned until eight tomorrow morning."

CHAPTER 17

Star Witness for the Prosecution

The next day, Assistant District Attorney Williams called her star witness to the stand: Vivian Lake. Allie had met the elder Ms. Lake a few times over the years. Allie had visited her best friend's home often, and they'd also had sleepovers. Allie was always amazed by Vivian's poise and beauty, a beauty that time never seemed to affect at all. Even though Ms. Lake was now pushing forty years old, Allie could perceive little change wrought by the intervening six years since she had last seen her.

Vivian Lake did not look at all like an older version of her daughter; she was taller and more slender, with gray eyes and long, straight, dark-brown hair (Cindy's eye color had come from her mother; her hair color came from the father she'd never known). Vivian attended the trial and wore a different designer outfit each day from her ultra-chic wardrobe. On the day of her testimony, Vivian chose a smart, navy-blue tailored suit, complemented by a pair of shoes with stiletto heels.

Ms. Lake traipsed to the witness stand when she was called, kittenishly sat down, and was sworn in. Vivian dutifully promised to tell "the truth, the whole truth, and nothing but the truth," but the "so help me God" part had long been removed from the oath, as had the practice of witnesses placing their left hands on the Holy Bible. After crossing her long, lean legs and adjusting her scandalously short skirt, the questioning began.

"Ms. Lake, could you please tell the court about your relationship with your daughter—that is, how it was prior to this year?" Ms. Williams said.

"Gladly. Even though I didn't actually raise my daughter, she and I were always quite close. We were almost more like sisters than mother and daughter. I taught my daughter to be a model—I mean a *paragon*. Obviously, I didn't teach her to be a model in terms of her profession. I didn't mean model in that sense of the word—"

Ms. Williams attempted to get her digressing witness back on track. "Please continue, Ms. Lake. You were saying that you taught your daughter to be a paragon ..."

"Ah, yes, how silly of me!" Ms. Lake giggled like a schoolgirl but then continued seriously. "I taught my daughter to be a paragon of postmodern society, to shun all such concepts as monogamy, purity, and abstinence. Most of all, I taught her to avoid anything to do with the accursed doctrines of Christianity."

Allie almost laughed at the Cindy's mother for equating Christianity with accursedness.

"In fact," Vivian Lake continued, "when Cynthia's best friend, Allie, first started spouting these ludicrous fables from that fairy-tale book called the *Bible*"—Ms. Lake said the word as if it left a bad taste in her mouth—"Cynthia and I both would laugh at her behind her back. And when I last saw my daughter, after doing my duty to instruct her in the conduct befitting a young lady, she was a thoroughly well-adjusted individual."

"And can you now tell this court, in your own words, what

you found when you visited your daughter in late February?" Ms. Williams requested.

"Gladly. Imagine my surprise when I returned a few years later to find that my own daughter had been reduced to a babbling idiot, spouting all manner of nonsense!"

"For instance?" Ms. Williams prompted.

"Objection. Counsel is leading the witness," Mr. Volk contended.

"Overruled," Judge Dawson said. "The witness will answer the question."

"Stuff like keeping herself 'pure until marriage' and 'second virginity'—whatever *that* means. Why would anyone even want *first* virginity? Now she wants to be a wife and a mother; she'd never wanted that before. She's started dressing even more conservatively and had the gall to tell me that I dressed immodestly!"

"And to what do you attribute these changes?" Ms. Williams asked.

"Objection. Calls for speculation on the part of the witness," Mr. Volk said.

"Sustained," Judge Dawson ruled. "However, as the defendant has already admitted her guilt in this matter, the court will stipulate that Ms. Allison Jane Holtz was in some way responsible for the changes in the younger Ms. Lake."

"Very well, Your Honor. No further questions," the ADA said.

"Court is recessed until one p.m.," Judge Dawson decided.

Following recess, Attorney Volk began his cross examination. "Mrs. Lake—"

"That's *Ms.* Lake," Vivian corrected him.

"Yes, it *is* Ms. Lake, isn't it?" Mr. Volk agreed knowingly. "The fact is, Ms. Lake, that you never married Cynthia's father. Isn't that correct?"

"Objection, Your Honor. Relevancy," Ms. Williams said.

"Your Honor, I am trying to establish this witness' unfitness as a mother."

"Sustained. Single motherhood is hardly an example of unfit parenting," Judge Dawson said.

Mr. Volk tried again. "Ms. Lake, you mentioned earlier that your daughter and you were once more like sisters."

"Yes," Vivian Lake replied with pride.

"Isn't this because you have never truly grown up?"

"Objection, Your Honor. The witness is not on trial here!" Ms. Williams said.

"Sustained. Watch yourself, Counselor," Judge Dawson warned.

Mr. Volk tried one last time. "Ms. Lake, you left your parents to raise your own daughter, and then you abandoned her altogether when she was only sixteen. Correct?"

"Objection, Your Honor. Relevancy," Ms. Williams repeated.

"Sustained," Judge Dawson concurred. "There is nothing suspect about a mother not raising her offspring or leaving the child once the child has reached legal age."

"And you only recently became a part of your daughter's life again, after an interval of nearly six years?" Mr. Volk continued.

"Objection, Your Honor. Same reason," ADA Williams said.

"Your Honor, I am trying to establish that Ms. Lake has not been a factor in her daughter's life for years and that she has never truly been a factor," Mr. Volk said.

"Objection sustained," Judge Dawson pronounced.

Mr. Volk thought for a moment, and then he asked the

witness, "Do you feel that your daughter was, at the age of sixteen, fully mature and capable of making her own decisions?"

"Yes, I do," Vivian Lake answered, but her voice betrayed that she took umbrage at the question.

"Then why do you doubt her ability, at the age of twenty-one, to make a major, life-changing decision, like deciding to become a Christian?"

"Objection. Calls for speculation on the part of the witness."

"Overruled. The witness will please answer the question," Judge Dawson said.

"*I* don't know!" Vivian Lake answered petulantly.

"One further question, Ms. Lake: do you contend that you have not seen any positive changes in your daughter following her conversion to Jesus Christ?"

"Well, she does seem nicer and more helpful than before," Vivian had to admit.

"No further questions, Your Honor," Mr. Volk concluded.

"Would the prosecution like to redirect?" Judge Dawson asked.

"Yes, Your Honor. Ms. Lake, would you say that you and your daughter are as close as you once were?" Ms. Williams asked her star witness.

"No, now she's always telling me that I'm a sinner and that I'm going to hell! What kind of daughter talks to her own mother like that?" Vivian exclaimed.

"No further questions, Your Honor," Ms. Williams said. "The prosecution rests."

"The witness may step down. Court is recessed until tomorrow at eight a.m."

Chapter 18

Can I Get a Witness?

The defense started presenting its case the next day. Mr. Volk began by calling Allie's family members to testify to her purity, her eternally good nature, and her civic uprightness. Ms. Williams did not have much to object to regarding most of these witnesses' testimonies; she didn't even cross-examine them. But when Jack Holtz took the stand, the ADA changed her strategy drastically.

"So, Mr. Holtz, you and your wife believe in the outmoded notion of maintaining chastity before marriage?" Ms. Williams sardonically inquired.

"Yes, we do," Jack stated firmly.

"And is this a practice to which you have *always* adhered? I mean, your wife looks rather far along in her pregnancy, considering the brief interval since your relatively recent marriage. Perhaps you two couldn't wait until your wedding day."

"Objection!" Mr. Volk exclaimed.

"I concur," the judge said. "That question was far out of bounds, Counselor. The objection is sustained. The jury will please disregard the last question."

Ms. Williams ceased her rather short cross-examination. "No further questions, Your Honor."

"Would the defense like to redirect?" Judge Dawson asked.

"Yes, Your Honor. Mr. Holtz, when were you and the defendant married?"

"Objection, Your Honor. Relevancy," the prosecutor said.

"Your Honor, the question is relevant to the prosecution's last question."

"But *my last* question was disregarded by the Honorable Judge Dawson," Ms. Williams pointed out.

"Your Honor, just because the jury has been ordered to disregard something doesn't negate that the jury has already heard it, thus planting suggestions in their minds," Lawyer Volk said.

"Overruled," the judge decided. "The witness will please answer the question."

"We were married on July 1 of last year," Jack answered.

"In other words, around ten months ago," Attorney Volk said. "And how far along is your wife in her pregnancy?"

"Objection, Your Honor. Relevancy again," the ADA said.

"Overruled," the judge repeated. "You opened the door on this one, Counselor."

"Less than a full eight months," Jack happily supplied.

"No further questions, Your Honor," Mr. Volk said.

"The witness may step down. Court is recessed until tomorrow at eight a.m."

The next day, the defense called Miss Cynthia Ann Lake.

Much murmuring ensued among the spectators in the courtroom, until the judge's gavel quieted them down. Miss Cynthia Ann Lake took the stand wearing a white blouse and a calf-length black skirt (even though she rarely wore skirts).

After she primly sat down on the witness stand, Judge Dawson asked the defense attorney, "Is the younger Ms. Lake being treated as a hostile witness?"

"No, Your Honor. Actually, Ms. Lake is my *star* witness," Mr. Volk replied.

"Objection, Your Honor," Ms. Williams said. "Having a daughter testify on the opposite side from her own mother in a court case is highly irregular."

"Your Honor, since my client is accused of corrupting the character of the younger Ms. Lake through her proselytizing, it is paramount for this court to determine if Miss Cynthia Ann Lake has truly been damaged through her exposure to Christianity."

"I agree," Judge Dawson said. "There is a precedent whereby a person cannot be forced to testify against a spouse, but the younger Ms. Lake is neither testifying against her mother nor being forced to testify, I assume. I will allow it."

After Cindy was sworn in, Mr. Volk began his direct examination.

"Miss Lake, could you please describe your life before your conversion to Christianity?"

"I was happy," Cindy replied.

Allie gulped, worried what Cindy might say, until her best friend continued.

"After all, they say ignorance is bliss."

"And what were you ignorant of?" Mr. Volk asked.

"Objection. Counsel is leading the witness," ADA Williams interrupted.

"Sustained," the judge ruled. "The witness will refrain from answering the question."

"Miss Lake, could you please describe, in your own words, your upbringing?" Mr. Volk asked.

"Yes, sir," Cindy answered. "My mother and my grandparents taught me to be a perfect model of progressive, postmodern society; to believe in evolution, in feminism, and in syncretism; and to believe that Christianity was the greatest evil in the history of the world. Because of my upbringing, I had no reason to think that my beliefs were wrong or that my behavior was sinful, except that …"

"Pray continue, Miss Lake," Attorney Volk said.

"Except that sometimes I would feel so *empty* inside, even though I followed everything that I'd ever been taught at home or at school regarding normal behavior. I stuffed these feelings of emptiness deep down inside by believing in my own divinity, as taught by the Worldwide Church of Syncretism."

"Were these feeling present even before Allison spoke to you regarding her faith?" Lawyer Volk asked.

"Yes, they were," Cindy answered after some thought, "but they got much worse after I reached my teens. After Allie got saved, as she called it, she would often tell me that my beliefs were wrong and that they were contradictory. Deep down, I knew that she was right. But I ignored what she said, and I continued to ignore my inner feelings as well. I mocked Allie's beliefs to assuage my guilty conscience. Outwardly, I would present a self-assured front, but inwardly, I wasn't as sure of myself as I acted."

"Could you please tell this court, in your own words, what transpired between Mrs. Allison Holtz and you last autumn?"

"You mean after I was raped on campus?" Cindy clarified.

"Objection, Your Honor. This trial is regarding the accused's proselytizing of this witness, not the alleged rape of this witness," the ADA said.

"Your Honor, I am trying to establish the emotional state of the witness at the time of the incident," Mr. Volk said.

The prosecutor quickly changed her mind. "Objection withdrawn, Your Honor."

"Very well then," a surprised Judge Dawson acknowledged. "Pray continue, Ms. Lake."

"Thank you, Your Honor. As I was saying, after I was released from the hospital following my rape, the Holtzes graciously put me up at their apartment so I wouldn't have to return to the scene of the crime, so to speak—the university coed dorms."

"And then what happened?" Mr. Volk asked.

"Objection. Counsel is leading the witness," Ms. Williams said with a sigh.

"Overruled. The witness will please answer the question," Judge Dawson said.

"Well, while I was staying with Jack and Allie, I was conflicted."

"Could you please elaborate?" the defense lawyer asked.

"On the one hand," Cindy said, "I thought that some of the Holtzes' beliefs were kind of strange."

"I'll bet!" Vivian Lake muttered.

"But on the other hand, I have never seen two people who were more in love with each other or who were more self-sacrificing toward each other. In the end, this is what made me listen to what they had to say about their religion—that and the fact that my rape disabused me of my long-held belief in the basic goodness of humankind."

"Ms. Lake, did you at any time feel as if you were being coerced to accept the Holtzes' religion?" Mr. Volk asked.

"No. After a while I really wanted whatever it was they possessed. In fact, I was the one who asked Allie how to become a Christian."

"And what occurred after your conversion?" Mr. Volk inquired.

"I felt a sense of peace. Finally, the tension that I felt from trying to live like a model citizen of our progressive, politically correct, postmodern society, and the emptiness that I felt while living this way was over."

"No further questions, Your Honor," Mr. Volk concluded.

"Your witness, Madam Prosecutor," Judge Dawson instructed.

"Thank you, Your Honor. Now, Ms. Lake, you mentioned your unfortunate rape earlier. Would it be fair to say that you were distraught at this point?"

"I suppose so."

"Then you would have been more susceptible to suggestion—say, to a certain religious belief system being forced upon you by your hosts?"

Now Allie and almost everyone else in the courtroom understood why the prosecutor had withdrawn her earlier objection regarding the mention of Cindy's rape.

"Objection, Your Honor. The witness has already testified that *she* was the one who initiated the conversation," Lawyer Volk said.

"Sustained. The witness will please disregard the question," the judge ruled.

"Now, while you were staying with the Holtzes, did Allison ever mention anything about gay marriage, or transgenders, or abortion?" Ms. Williams asked.

"Objection. Relevancy, Your Honor," Mr. Volk said.

"Your Honor, I am trying to establish the fact that Ms. Holtz has a total disregard for the law and rampant intolerance toward anyone who believes differently from her."

"Objection overruled. The witness will please answer the question."

Cindy hesitated.

Judge Dawson became impatient. "The witness will answer the question or risk being cited with contempt of court!"

"Yes. Allie did make comments about such things from time to time," Cindy answered.

"And what *was* her opinion of these things?" Ms. Williams pressed.

"I got the feeling that she was not in favor of them," Cindy admitted reluctantly. Then she looked over at her best friend and mouthed the word *sorry*.

Ms. Williams ended her cross-examination. "No further questions, Your Honor."

"Would the defense like to redirect?" Judge Dawson offered.

"Yes, Your Honor. Ms. Lake, you mentioned earlier that you were, in some ways, happy before your conversion to Christ."

"Yes, sir."

"And how do you feel now?" Mr. Volk asked.

"Now I'm ecstatic!" Cindy rejoiced. "I'm *so* much happier than I was before I accepted Jesus Christ as my personal Savior!"

"No further questions, Your Honor," Mr. Volk finished.

"The witness may step down. Court is adjourned until Monday morning at eight o'clock," Judge Dawson announced.

CHAPTER 19

Christian Testimony

The next Monday morning, Attorney Volk called his final witness, Mrs. Allison Jane Holtz.

Allie, wearing an emerald-green maternity dress, got up with great difficulty (and with her loving husband's help) and waddled to the witness stand. Once she gingerly took her seat, the bailiff instructed her to raise her right hand (though she was not told to place her left hand on the Holy Bible; in fact, there were no Bibles present in the courtroom, other than the ones that had been smuggled in by the defendant and her supporters). Then the bailiff intoned in a somber voice:

"Do you solemnly swear to tell the truth, the whole truth, and nothing but the truth?"

"I swear," Allie said, and then she added, "So help me God."

The judge officially reminded the defendant of the protocol. "Invoking the name of God is no longer necessary during these proceedings, Ms. Holtz."

Allie acknowledged his words with a quick nod of her head, while inwardly wondering how any witness could be trusted to tell the truth under such conditions. Then she gave her full attention to her lawyer as he began his questioning.

"Mrs. Holtz, could you please tell this court, in your own words, about your life before your conversion?"

"Objection, Your Honor. Relevancy," ADA Williams said.

"Overruled," Judge Dawson said, even before Mr. Volk could argue his case. "The witness will please answer the question."

"I grew up a fairly normal child, happy for the most part," Allie said, "at least until I turned twelve years old, when my father died of cancer."

"And how did his death affect you?" Mr. Volk asked.

"Objection, Your Honor. Counsel is leading the witness," Ms. Williams claimed.

"Not in my estimation," the judge said. "Objection overruled. The witness will please answer the question."

It seemed to Allie that the prosecutor was grasping at straws. *That's a good sign*, she thought. "I'd always been a happy-go-lucky child," Allie answered, "but my personality changed somewhat after my father's death. I became much more serious about life."

"And were you a particularly religious child?"

"Not at all. None of my family was religious until my father—and then my mother—accepted Jesus Christ as their personal Lord and Savior after reading a copy of the New Testament that Mom found in Second-Hand News, a used-book store. Reading the Gospels made me realize as well that Jesus Christ was the Son of God and that He was crucified for the sins of the world, so I accepted Jesus Christ too, and—"

"Objection!" the assistant district attorney exclaimed. "Must the court endure the defendant's preposterous religious views?"

Allie could tell that the prosecutor wasn't merely doing her job; it was clear she had an intense hatred for the truth of the gospel of Jesus Christ.

"Sustained," Judge Dawson ruled. "Let's move it along, Counselor."

"Yes, Your Honor." Counselor Volk then asked his client, "And what happened following your conversion to Christianity?"

"Just like my parents, I was flooded with joy and peace. I immediately told all of my friends about it. Naturally, I wanted to tell everybody about the joy that I'd found."

"Mrs. Holtz, why did you invite Ms. Lake into your home?"

"Cindy didn't want to go back to the dorms after what happened to her, understandably so."

"Did you have any ulterior motive behind this act, such as converting her to your faith?"

"No. I thought that Cindy would never come to have faith in Christ. She seemed so close-minded toward the gospel. I actually hadn't witnessed to Cindy in years, not until that night, when she asked me about my faith."

"No further questions, Your Honor," Mr. Volk said.

"Court is recessed until one p.m.," Judge Dawson declared.

Following the recess, Assistant District Attorney Williams began her cross-examination.

"Ms. Holtz, you claim that you became a Christian shortly after your father's untimely death."

"Yes, ma'am," Allie confirmed.

"That's Ms. Williams. I'm not married," she corrected Allie.

"Yes, Ms. Williams," Allie said. Then she cheekily added, "And while we're on the subject, it's Mrs. Holtz, not Ms. I *am* married."

"Counselor Volk, please instruct your client to afford this court the proper respect," Judge Dawson requested.

"Yes, Your Honor," Counselor Volk answered.

"Pray continue, Madam Prosecutor," the judge instructed.

"Yes, Your Honor. Mrs. Holtz, since your conversion followed so closely after your father's death, are you absolutely certain that it wasn't only an emotional decision on your part?"

"Objection, Your Honor. Relevancy," Mr. Volk objected.

"Sustained," Judge Dawson ruled. "The purpose of these proceedings is to determine whether or not the defendant is guilty of proselytizing and criminal political incorrectness, not to determine if her religious views are correct or genuine."

"Very well, Your Honor," Ms. Williams acknowledged. "Mrs. Holtz, you mentioned before that your conversion was the result of reading a Bible found in Second-Hand News."

"Yes, but actually, my conversion was the result of the work of the Holy Spirit."

"Then I suppose that you would be aggrieved to know that the proprietor of Second-Hand News is currently in prison for the crime of proselytizing."

Allie *was* aggrieved to learn this fact, and she was shocked by the malicious glee the prosecutor displayed in dispensing the disturbing information.

"Objection!" Allie's attorney exclaimed, jumping to his feet. "Is it the state's normal practice to employ scare tactics on defendants?"

"Sustained," Judge Dawson agreed. "Another example of similar courtroom shenanigans, and I'll have a discussion with you in my chambers, Ms. Williams."

"Yes, Your Honor," Ms. Williams answered with mock contriteness. Then she changed tactics. "Ms. Holtz—that is, *Mrs.* Holtz, what are your views on the subjects of abortion, homosexual marriage, transgender rights—"

"Objection, Your Honor. The prosecutor already asked this question of my previous witness," Mr. Volk pointed out.

"Your Honor, I feel it's important to hear it directly from the accused's own mouth," ADA Williams contended.

"Overruled. The defendant will please answer the question," the judge instructed.

"I believe …" Allie hesitated; then she gathered up her courage and answered confidently. "I believe that those practices are against God's law."

"Even though they are all legal, according to US law?" Ms. Williams taunted.

"We ought to obey God rather than men," Allie said, quoting Acts 5:29.

The assistant district attorney smiled triumphantly at this admission. "So, Mrs. Holtz, you fully admit that you have no respect for the law whatsoever—"

"Objection, Your Honor. Counsel is generalizing," Mr. Volk contended.

"Sustained," Judge Dawson ruled. "The prosecution will please stick to the facts."

"Very well, Your Honor. Let me amend my last question. Mrs. Holtz, do you have disregard for only some of the laws of this state but not all of them?"

"*Only* the laws that contradict God's word," Allie said.

"Oh, so you feel that you can decide willy-nilly which laws to obey and which to disregard?"

"Even though I don't agree with these laws, that doesn't mean that I actively discriminate against the people who practice these things," Allie stated.

"But you pass judgment on them, like, for instance, Ms. Charlene Lang."

"I wasn't passing judgment on her. I simply used the wrong

pronoun because I was confused. It was the first time that I'd met her after her change."

"But you have made many other similar slips of the tongue over the years, haven't you, Mrs. Holtz? I have documentation on it. I could have called a multitude of witnesses to testify against you regarding this matter."

"Your Honor, the prosecution is badgering the defendant!" Mr. Volk complained.

"Agreed. Ms. Williams, you have made your point. Move on."

"Very well, Your Honor. Mrs. Holtz, your religion instructs you not to bear false witness; isn't that right?"

"Yes, Ms. Williams, it does," Allie answered evenly.

"Then you are being absolutely truthful when you state that you did *not* invite Ms. Lake into your home to convert her to your intolerant religion?"

"Objection, Your Honor. This was already covered in my direct examination," Mr. Volk reminded the court.

"Sustained. The defendant will disregard the question."

"One more question, Mrs. Holtz. You mentioned earlier that you—and I quote—'wanted to tell everybody' about the joy you'd found. Given the same circumstances as you had with Ms. Lake last year, if someone else asked you about your religion, outside of the confines of a church building, would you once again share your faith with that person?"

Allie knew that admitting this would surely seal her fate.

"Let me remind you that you are under oath," Ms. Williams said.

"Yes, I would," Allie admitted truthfully. "I would if it would bring peace to that person's life."

The courtroom broke out in murmurs.

Judge Dawson forcefully banged her gavel. "Order in the court!"

"No further questions, Your Honor," ADA Williams said.

"Would the defense like to redirect this witness?" Judge Dawson asked.

"Yes, Your Honor. Mrs. Holtz, do you hate transsexuals like Charlene Lang?"

"No. I don't hate anybody, not even people with whom I strongly disagree. I just can't keep straight all of the correct gender designations anymore."

This statement brought some chuckles from the spectators.

"Order in the court, or I will clear this courtroom!" Judge Dawson warned.

"No further questions, Your Honor," Mr. Volk said. "The defense rests."

"Please step down," Judge Dawson directed Allie. "Court is adjourned until tomorrow morning at eight o'clock."

CHAPTER 20

Sober Judgment

The next morning was the day for closing arguments. The prosecution led off.

"Entities of the jury"—*Ladies and gentlemen* of the jury had long since been dispensed with for being too exclusive, and even the word *people* was now considered offensive to some prospective jurors—"while observing the defendant, the diminutive, delicate, and obviously pregnant Mrs. Allison Jane Holtz, you may be tempted to regard her with pity, but I would caution you not to do so. The accused may be all of these things, but she is also a lawbreaker. She has broken the laws against proselytizing and criminal political incorrectness. You may not think that these are serious offenses; you may not even agree with these laws, but the law is still the law, and Mrs. Allison Jane Holtz has broken the law. Thank you."

Next, Defense Attorney Brian Volk made his appeal to the jury.

"Ladies and gentlemen of the jury—or variations thereof, yes, my client has broken those two laws; she has freely admitted to it. But the pertinent question before us today is whether or not there should even be laws of this nature. The framers of the Constitution, in response to the state-run churches of

Europe, explicitly mandated that no government would be able to rule over the church. I quote: 'Congress shall make no law respecting an establishment of religion, or prohibiting the free exercise thereof.'

"The original intent of this clause was to protect freedom of religion in this country, but it has been hijacked by liberal lawmakers and activist judges as a way of ensuring freedom from religion. One of the tenets of the Christian faith is to share the good news of the gospel, but if the state of Minnesota and other 'progressive' states like it had their way, Christians like Mrs. Allison Holtz would have to be content with preaching to the choir and not reaching anyone who actually needs to hear that news.

"It may be that 'backward' Christians like me are only cursing the dark with regards to this issue; that similar laws to the ones that have been newly instituted here and that have long been on the books on both the East and the West Coasts will eventually be enacted in every state of the union. But while I yet have breath within me, I will fight these unconstitutional and—dare I say it?—intolerant laws. But one has to wonder why the Christian religion draws most of the ire of the liberal rulers of this country.

"Is it because true biblical Christianity is a threat to their politically correct policies? Or perhaps it's the fact that our faith, which instructs us to love our enemies, makes us such an easy target. After all, it's a lot safer to persecute individuals who aren't going to retaliate by declaring jihad against you! And why is it that Muslim terrorists can blow people up, but Islam is still called a religion of peace, while nonviolent Christians are branded as haters, only because they won't support the liberal agenda?

"But enough of my personal soapbox, I am here to represent

one particular Christian: a young lady by the name of Allison Jane Holtz. Allie Holtz, contrary to what the ADA has implied throughout this trial, is *not* a hater. She doesn't hate homosexuals, transsexuals, or heterosexuals, for that matter. She loves people, even the people who are persecuting her. She loved her best friend, Miss Cynthia Ann Lake, enough to tell her, when asked, how she could gain peace with God.

"Cynthia Lake has testified to how empty she felt before Jesus Christ came into her life. Now she is fulfilled, even joyful. She is not complaining about Allie's proselytizing to her. The complaint was lodged by Cynthia's mother, a woman who, by her own admission, was absent from her young daughter's life for nearly six years! Why should Allison Holtz be punished for helping her best friend? Why should she be considered public enemy number one for performing a loving act?

"The ADA warned you not to take pity on the defendant. But I am begging you to do so. Allison Jane Holtz is a twenty-one-year-old woman with her entire life ahead of her. She is a newlywed, married for not quite a full year. Most important, Allie is an expectant mother, only weeks away from giving birth to her first child. Do not ruin the life of an innocent person, much less the life of her innocent unborn child, by incarcerating a guileless young woman. I am entreating you to return a verdict of not guilty for my client. Thank you."

Ms. Williams then got up and gave her rebuttal. "Obviously, Mr. Volk is an impassioned speaker who likes to tug at a jury's heartstrings. But he is incorrect on a few of his facts. First of all, the state of Minnesota does adhere to the First Amendment of the Constitution. Persons of faith are allowed the free exercise of their religion, as long as they exercise it within a church building. But radical Christians like Allison Jane Holtz are not content with that; they won't be happy until they have converted everyone to their irrational, outdated, hateful religion.

"Lawyer Volk is also wrong when he refers to his deluded client as an innocent, guileless person. She is a lawbreaker and a troublemaker. Worse of all, she is a hater! It's about time that someone sends a message to these fanatical Christians that we are not going to tolerate their narrow-minded beliefs anymore! That someone is *you*, entities of the jury. I am asking—nay, I am demanding that you return with the guilty verdict, which Mrs. Allison Jane McAllister Holtz so richly deserves. Thank you."

After Judge Dawson gave her instructions to the jury, they were sequestered, and the court was adjourned, pending the outcome of the jury's deliberations.

A few days later, after waiting on tenterhooks, Allie and her supporters were informed that the jury reached a decision. Once the interested parties had assembled in the courtroom, the verdict phase of the trial began. The jury foreman handed a piece of paper to the bailiff, who in turn handed it to the judge. After she read the verdict, the paper was then handed back to the bailiff, who handed it back to the jury foreman. Judge Dawson then rhetorically asked the jury foreman, "Has the jury reached a verdict in this case?"

"Yes, we have, Your Honor," the foreman answered.

"Would the defendant please rise for the reading of the verdict?" Judge Dawson said.

The defendant complied—with much difficulty.

"On the first count of the indictment, regarding the crime of proselytizing, how does the jury find the defendant?"

"We, the jury, find the defendant, Ms. Allison Jane McAllister Holtz, guilty as charged, Your Honor."

The verdict caused quite a commotion in the courtroom, with the spectators displaying either triumph or dismay. Allie held on to the railing in front of her and only barely managed not to swoon over the jury's decision.

"And on the second count of the indictment, regarding the crime of criminal political incorrectness, how does the jury find the defendant?" Judge Dawson asked.

"We, the jury, find the defendant, Ms. Allison Jane McAllister Holtz, guilty as charged, Your Honor."

Allie began to weep softly, as Judge Dawson addressed her.

"Mrs. Allison Jane McAllister Holtz, you have been found guilty of your crimes in a court of law. You will now be escorted to the state penitentiary, where you will await sentencing."

Allie was led away amid much weeping from her party. She barely had time to kiss her loving husband and to whisper goodbye to him. She was then hauled off to the state prison, where she would wait and hope that the judge would show her leniency—and that Judge Dawson wouldn't take too long to come to that decision.

⚖

Allie didn't have to wait long for the sentencing; she was back in the same courtroom (this time, manacled and dressed in an orange jumpsuit) the very next day. Judge Dawson addressed the courtroom.

"As a courtesy, I will save Mrs. Holtz the discomfort of standing during my remarks. In coming to my decision, there were many factors to consider. First of all, this is her first offense, and second, Mrs. Holtz's conduct has been exemplary in all other ways regarding the laws of the state of Minnesota, save those laws that pertain to the offenses of which she has been convicted. And there were many other mitigating circumstances in this case.

"As to the first count, there was very little hope of an acquittal, as the defendant freely admitted her guilt. The vagueness of the law regarding proselytizing is, however, regrettable. It is unclear whether or not a person is guilty of the crime if the other party solicits the information. In this particular case, however, as Ms. Lake was of legal age at the time of the incident, and she seems pleased with the results of her conversion, the complaint brought by the elder Ms. Lake is unfounded.

"As to the second count of the indictment, while the defendant displays many subversive ideas that are indicative of her Christian faith, there seems to be no malice in her opinions, and her beliefs have not caused her to act in discriminatory ways toward any protected classes. As yet, the government has not instituted laws outlawing what George Orwell termed as 'thought crime,' so while many of Mrs. Holtz's beliefs are prejudicial, they do not constitute as criminal, at least not in *my* judicial opinion."

Judge Dawson's remarks allowed Allie to begin to get her hopes up regarding the outcome of her sentencing hearing.

"The prisoner will now stand for the sentencing," Judge Dawson then ordered.

Allie managed to raise herself to a standing position, and then she waited with bated breath for the judge's pronouncement.

"It is my judgment that the convicted, Mrs. Allison Jane Holtz, be placed on probation for a period of not less than three years—"

The jubilation of Allie and her people temporarily interrupted the judge's decision. When order was once again restored in the courtroom, Judge Dawson instructed the convicted felon, saying, "The conditions of your probation are as follows: (1) You will be required to meet with a probation officer on a weekly basis; (2) You are not to leave the state of Minnesota during the *entire* period of your probation; and (3) You are not to proselytize outside the bounds of a church building for the duration of your probation. And in my judgment, you would do well not to proselytize outside of church even *after* your probation.

"In the future, Mrs. Holtz, I would advise you that if anyone asks you about your faith, you simply ask them to meet you at a legally recognized church building within the state of Minnesota to discuss the matter further. Failure to obey *any* of these dictates will result in prison time," Judge Dawson sternly warned the grateful malefactor, and then the judge banged her gavel soundly. "The business of this court is now concluded. Court is adjourned."

After kissing her husband and hugging her mother, her brother, Cindy, and Mr. Volk, Allie Holtz waddled out of the courtroom, and, after exchanging her prison garb for her maternity clothes, she waddled out of the courthouse, if not actually as an innocent person then at least no longer an incarcerated one.

Chapter 21

Special Delivery

The next day, Allie's grateful family—Jack, Billie Jo, and Rod—and her only friend, Cindy, threw her a Not Going Away to Prison party at the McAllister home. Also in attendance was Mr. Brian Volk.

Sometime during the proceedings, Allie told her attorney, "Thank you for representing me in court, Mr. Volk."

"Don't thank me. I lost the case, remember? I'm only thankful to God that the judge showed you mercy. As it was, that entire trial was a miscarriage of justice."

Allie simply looked down at her bloated belly and replied, "Then let's all pray that it's the only miscarriage I will have to endure."

The Holtz-McAllister clan's prayers were answered, and Allie gave birth to a healthy baby girl on June 8, a little premature and a little underweight (barely five pounds), but despite the dire warnings of both Allie's doctor and her obstetrician, there were no birth defects—the baby didn't even need an incubator. Thankfully, the baby did not live up to her astrological sign of Gemini, and Allie bore only one child, rather than giving birth to twins in the Twin Cities.

It was not the easiest of births, but Allie survived her travail and was rewarded for her labor (literally) with a beautiful baby girl. The mother then was wheeled into her room and propped up in bed, and the baby was cleaned up and gently placed in her mother's waiting arms. Allie lovingly cradled her newborn child, and she softly spoke to her husband, who was standing at her bedside.

"Isn't she beautiful?" Allie murmured in wonderment of God's special delivery to them.

"Yes," Jack agreed as he leaned over to kiss his wife's cheek. "She has your beautiful face, I do believe."

"I don't know about that," Allie demurred, "but she certainly appears to have inherited my red hair. Thank you, Jack, for being with me every step of the way."

"I will never leave thee, nor forsake thee," Jack quoted. "I vowed to stay with you through better or worse. We have already survived the worst part; this part definitely constitutes the better."

"There may very well be even worse parts coming," Allie said seriously, "with the way this world is going."

"Then we'll face it together," Jack promised.

"Yes, we will—Jack, Allie, and Cynthia Josephine Holtz, God's special delivery!"

"And baby makes three," Jack said.

"And the Lord makes four," Allie reminded her husband. "With God on our side, how could we possibly fail?"

The Holtzes brought baby Cindy Jo home after a few days, and Allie spent her time taking care of her newborn, interspersed with keeping her weekly appointments with her probation officer. Thanks to her newfound (yet unwanted) celebrity, she was often asked about her Christian faith, and she always offered to discuss the matter in an official church setting; some people would take her up on it. Most of them did not, and Allie suspected that those who didn't were probably trying to entrap her.

Once Rod McAllister finished his college degree in law, he began to represent other victims of Minnesota's intolerant anti-Christian laws. Cindy became a psychologist and decided to remain in the ready-made mission field that was Minnesota, and Rod and Cindy eventually married each other and settled down in Minneapolis. Most important, with the Holy Spirit's help, the happy couple had a God-honoring marriage, and they both lived godly lives.

After Allie's probation ended and Jack had completed his college education in law enforcement, the Holtz family decided to stay in Minnesota as well. Billie Jo McAllister also remained in the North Star State; she wanted to be in close proximity so she could spoil her new granddaughter rotten. She remained a certified public accountant as well. Jack became a police officer, and Allie opted to be a stay-at-home mom and to raise her child in the "nurture and the admonition of the Lord."

Part II

The Children of Disobedience

Children, obey your parents in the Lord: for this is right.

—Ephesians 6:1
(The epistle of Paul the apostle)

Wherein in time past ye walked according to the course of this world, according to the prince of the power of the air, the spirit that now worketh in the children of disobedience.

—Ephesians 2:2
(The epistle of Paul the apostle)

CHAPTER 22

Red Headed Blackmailer

"**I**f I don't get my way ..." Cynthia Josephine Holtz threatened, with her arms crossed and a determined look upon her relatively young face. Then she thought of the perfect threat. "If I don't get my way, I'll tell Principal Nye on you!"

Allie Holtz's face changed from red with anger (as a result of the latest heated argument with her headstrong daughter) to pale white. "W-what will you tell her?" Mrs. Holtz asked in an unsteady voice.

"I'll her everything! I'll tell her about the Bible reading, the praying. I'll tell her about all of the Christian stuff that you make me do against my will!" Allie's daughter smirked triumphantly as she watched her mother's face grow even paler than before. She had really scored with that one.

"Now, Cindy Jo, you know that we have never forced our religion on you," Allie argued.

"That's a matter of opinion. And the name is *Josephine!*"

Cynthia Josephine was young Miss Holtz's given name (a combination of Allie's best friend, Cynthia Lake's, first name, and an alteration of Allie's mother, Billie Jo McAllister's, middle name), but she had answered to Cynthia, Cindy, or even Cindy Jo for years. It was only recently that she had come to regard

Josephine as a much more mature and regal-sounding name. Now that Cynthia Josephine Holtz had recently reached the exalted age of thirteen, she felt that she was all grown up.

Cynthia Josephine Holtz was a very small, slender girl with dark gray eyes, freckles, and long, flaming-red hair. With each succeeding generation, the hair color of the women of the O'Brien/McAllister/Holtz family seemed to grow progressively darker. Cynthia Jo's grandmother's hair was strawberry blonde, and her mother's hair was closer to orange in color, but Cindy Jo's hair was a deep, dark red.

Josephine (or Cynthia, Cindy Jo, or whatever name that she chose to self-identify) pressed her advantage even further. "If you don't let me go to the movies with my friends, I'll even tell the principal that you and Daddy have spanked me!"

An even worse crime to the progressive powers that be than parents foisting their religious beliefs upon their own children was the practice of corporal punishment. It was true that the Holtzes, in the past, had to resort to applying the board of education to the seat knowledge on more than one occasion while rearing their willful daughter, after other forms of coercion had failed. They had only employed this method of childrearing in the face of their daughter's flagrant defiance, but she had often proved to be quite the defiant child.

Going to movies with her godless friends was only the latest bone of contention between Josephine and her long-suffering parents. The liberal indoctrination and sex and violence that passed for entertainment propagated by Hollywood had not gotten any better over the years. Added to this was that the rating system had long since been dispensed with, except in the case of X-rated material. Parental guidance was no longer suggested; it wasn't even allowed.

Still, the Holtzes at least tried to keep their young,

impressionable daughter away from the worse cinematic offenders that came from Tinseltown. The latest example of the film industry's preoccupation with the ongoing slasher/splatter film revival that Cynthia was just dying to see definitely qualified as the worst! Even the disturbing images displayed in the TV ads for the film ("Just when you thought it was safe to go back to the bathroom—*Blood Bath II*, the sequel!") were enough to make Allie feel ill.

Now Allison Jane Holtz was in a quandary. Over thirteen years ago, when she was a young college student, she had boldly faced jail time for the crime of sharing her Christian faith. But now that she was on the back side of thirty, she didn't know if she could go through all of that again. Her fear wasn't only that she could lose her freedom over the charge; she could also lose her daughter too. The state had taken away other parents' children for far less of an offense than this.

Obviously, Mrs. Holtz was painfully aware that she was, in a sense, already losing her daughter to the world. At one time, Cynthia Josephine's relationship with her parents wasn't so fraught with tension. In the beginning, little Cindy Jo Holtz had been a reasonably attentive and obedient child, though she was always strong-willed. As she drew closer to adolescence, she grew ever increasingly argumentative and rebellious. But it was much worse than that.

It was only recently that Mr. and Mrs. Holtz realized, much to their mutual dismay, that their daughter had never really shared their Christian faith. Cynthia had only pretended to be a believer in order to keep in her parents' good graces. Laboring under the delusion that their daughter was truly saved, Mom and Dad Holtz had tried to appeal to Cindy's Christian conscience.

Then one day a few months ago, after she turned thirteen

years old, during another heated argument, their daughter had blurted out, "But I'm *not* a Christian! I've never been a Christian! I only told you what I knew you wanted to hear!"

As much as the Holtzes would've liked to believe that this provocative statement was only another example of their daughter's fiery Irish temper (her grandmother's maiden name had been O'Brien), it soon became apparent to the parents that she had meant every word. And Jo had spent the past few months punctuating that statement by acting like a holy terror (or, to be more accurate, an unholy terror)—willful, obstinate, and intractable. She pole-vaulted over every boundary that her parents set for her and demanded her wayward way at every turn.

Thus, after deciding that a movie—even one as potentially violent and disturbing as *Blood Bath II* promised to be—was not a hill that she was prepared to die upon, Allie Holtz relented with a sigh.

"All right, Josephine, you win—this time. You may go to this horrible horror movie. Just don't come crying to me when you have nightmares about it."

Josephine Holtz went to see *Blood Bath II* with her friends. She spent most of the ninety-minute movie screaming in abject terror, with her quivering hands covering her shocked eyes. And she did have a number of horrible nightmares over the next several weeks as a result of having watched the movie. But she never once gave her mother the satisfaction of running to her for succor following a frightful dream.

Chapter 23

Ill-Conceived

For his part, Mr. Jack Holtz was none too happy with his wife's swift capitulation of her principles in the matter of their disobedient daughter's choice of movie viewing. But eventually, even he had to agree that they should pick their battles carefully with their incorrigible daughter. And now everything seemed to be a battle royal with Josephine. In fact, other than enacting the procedure prescribed in Deuteronomy 21:18–21, Jack was at a loss for what to do with their rebellious offspring.

It pained both parents to see the recent changes in their once-innocent (albeit not always obedient) little girl. It was almost like someone had snatched up their Christian daughter one night and replaced her with an evil changeling. The possibility of demon possession had been seriously considered. Jack had even tried an exorcism, but that only resulted in Josephine's laughing in her hapless father's face and then gaily skipping out of the room. The truth was that Josephine didn't actually have a demon; she just didn't possess the Holy Spirit.

At first, Cynthia Josephine Holtz had been a sweet child and a religious one as well. She had listened to her parents' stories about Noah's ark, Daniel in the lions' den, and David and Goliath. She dutifully read her children's Bible daily, and she prayed before meals and before bedtime. She saw no reason to question her parents' Christian faith. In fact, she had entered Open Minds Elementary School in Minneapolis, Minnesota, as a child who loved, honored, and obeyed her parents.

But the progressive public school system seemed intent on molding students into its own image. The teachers and administrators at Open Minds Elementary believed that they knew what was best for the children, not the children's parents. The first volley was when Cindy was sent to the principal's office for praying in school, which consisted of her bowing her head, folding her hands, and praying silently before eating her lunch; she learned not be so demonstrative in saying grace in the future.

But thanks to her elementary school's indoctrination for seven hours a day, five days a week (versus the significantly less time that her parents had to instruct her), Cindy Jo Holtz eventually began to consider what her teachers were constantly hammering into her little head: that the Holy Bible was simply a collection of fairy tales and that evolution was a scientific fact; that humankind was only the result of time plus chance, just another animal, and definitely not made in the image of God.

Besides the scholastic bombardment upon little Cindy Jo Holtz, there was the social pressure. Cynthia liked being liked, and the constant ridicule she received from her fellow students (and even some of her teachers) at Open Minds Elementary School as a result of her Christian beliefs was excruciating. Her chief tormentor and nemesis had been a girl in the same grade, named Taylor Nye. Miss Nye was a popular girl, owing in no small part to being a beneficiary of the nepotism of her mother.

Bobbie Nye had been the biology teacher at Barack Obama High School for many years (where she was both a popular teacher with her students and in the good graces of her employers) before she went into administration. She was currently the principal at Our (First) Lady Hillary Rodham Clinton Middle School. Besides this, the younger Ms. Nye was something of a local celebrity owing to two factors. The first was that her mother was said to be a distant descendant of Bill Nye, the Science Guy.

The second aspect was that not only did Taylor Nye have two mommies, but she was one of the first children in the entire country who was born as the result of artificial fertilization. A few years earlier, modern science had found a way to induce pregnancy in women without any contribution from men whatsoever (no insemination required, artificial or otherwise). This particular immaculate conception only produced female offspring, but it allowed lesbian couples to reproduce sans male members of the species.

Taylor had been raised by Bobbie and her lawfully wedded wife, Joyce. Thanks to her long, straight, yellow-blonde hair, most people who didn't know any better assumed that Bobbie was Taylor's natural mother (if anything associated with Taylor's birth could be called natural). It was an assumption that Taylor didn't bother to correct, owing to the fame that it brought her. It was only when she reached puberty that people noticed that Taylor's nose held a resemblance to Joyce's prominent proboscis.

Taylor Nye was one of the in-crowd at Open Minds. Besides her rumored famous heritage and her miracle birth (though progressive society would never use such a Christian word as *miracle*), she was also a pretty enough girl (her nose and the braces on her teeth notwithstanding), with long, golden-blonde hair and pretty gray eyes. This meant that she was particularly popular with her male classmates. And to the mild disappointment of her mothers, Taylor did not share her parents' orientation.

Taylor had been overjoyed to learn that one of her classmates was a Christian (they were so rare these days). Like most popular students, Taylor received her chief pleasure in bullying the unpopular students, and in the current sociopolitical climate, nobody was more unpopular than Christians. At Open Minds Elementary School, bullying Christians was a favorite pastime of many, since the teachers at the school turned a blind eye. As long as they stopped short of physical violence, it was open season on the hapless (and helpless) young Christians.

Young Ms. Nye took every opportunity to needle and bait her quarry.

"So, Cindy the Christian, is it really true that you believe that instead of evolving from apes, humankind was formed from the dust of the ground by some mythical god? In that case, you'd better watch your step when you go outside, or you might step on one of your ancestors!"

Or any time that it rained, Taylor would say something like, "Uh-oh, it looks like Holy Holtz's loving yet vengeful God is raining down His judgment upon us again! Is your family going to build a new ark, collect all the animals two by two, and leave the rest of us sinners to sink or swim in another worldwide flood?"

Cindy the Christian grew so tired of the abuse that one day she said, "I'm not really a Christian. It's more my parents who believe in all that stuff."

Eleven-year-old Cindy Jo Holtz felt guilty after saying that, not so much because it was a lie, as she honestly didn't know what she believed in anymore, but because she felt like she was betraying her loving parents.

Taylor smirked. "Maybe there's hope for you yet, Cindy Jo Christian."

Chapter 24

Sleeping (Over) with the Enemy

Eventually, Cindy Jo found it easier to swim with the tide than to swim against it. So she kept her mouth shut on spiritual matters, stopped praying before her meals in the lunchroom, and she said (or regurgitated on the tests) whatever her teachers wanted to hear. She also told her parents at home what she knew they wanted to hear, and for a few months, she led a double life. Cynthia Josephine Holtz's downward slide toward apostasy was a gradual one, but it was a genuine one nevertheless.

By the time Cindy was in the middle of seventh grade, Taylor Nye did an about-face and teased her less and less. But Cindy's life got even easier one day when Taylor and her gang ganged up on another Christian student, and Cindy joined in on the fun. From that time on, Taylor treated her differently. She even took Cindy under her merciless wing. Soon the tormented became the tormentor, and Miss Holtz found that, as far as abuse was concerned, it was more enjoyable to give than to receive.

Cindy (or Josephine, as she now thought of herself) even began bullying her own cousin, Rose McAllister (Uncle Rod and Aunt Cindy's daughter) on the school bus. Previous to this, the first cousins had been close, and Josephine could tell that her nine-year-old cousin was hurt by her traitorous act. But Josephine was quite willing to sacrifice this familial relationship for the new one she now enjoyed with Taylor Nye.

If only that pesky verse that she'd learned as a child didn't keep coming to her mind every time that she bullied one of her fellow Christians (if Josephine even was a Christian): "Saul, Saul, why persecutest thou me?" But eventually, Josephine's conscience became "seared with a hot iron," and her guilty feelings lessened and lessened until they ceased altogether.

Soon, the two school friends were as thick as thieves. A real coup for Josephine was when her newfound friend invited her over to the Nye house one day near the end of their seventh-grade year for a sleepover. Josephine was ecstatic (or at least she was until it was time to ask her parents for their permission).

"Of course we are pleased that you are making new friends at school," Mrs. Holtz replied (although *a* friend at school would've been more accurate), "but we really don't know anything about this … Taylor, did you say her name was?"

"Yes, her name is Taylor," Josephine said.

"And what is her last name?" Mr. Holtz inquired.

"Um … Nye," Josephine nervously supplied.

Allie gasped. "As in Bobbie Nye's daughter?"

"Yes," Josephine confirmed, even more nervously.

"I'm not at all comfortable with you becoming friends with Bobbie Nye's unnaturally conceived daughter," Jack Holtz said.

"I agree. I'm *sure* this girl will be a bad influence on you," Allie added.

"First Corinthians 15:33—'Be not deceived: evil communications corrupt good manners,'" Jack quoted.

"But how can we be a good influence on unbelievers if we never have any contact with them?" Josephine argued (though this was only a smoke screen; she had no intention of trying to influence her new friend for the good).

"You're not going to try to witness to her, are you?" her mother asked worriedly. "You *know* about the anti-proselytizing law."

"I doubt that the authorities would press a suit against a middle-schooler," Jack said. "Besides, we can't keep silent and let everyone else go to hell."

"You're right," Allie conceded, "but she might end up in juvie hall, and I wouldn't want even that for our daughter."

"She's going to have to stand up for her faith eventually."

Sensing that the debate was derailing from the original topic, Josephine tried to get her parents' trains of thought back on track. "I'm not going to witness to her yet. I just want to start by befriending her."

"That's a good first step," Jack agreed. "You have our permission then."

Allie still wasn't sure that she was comfortable with having their precious daughter sleeping behind enemy lines (so to speak) with the daughter of her atheistic former biology teacher, but she honored her husband's headship in the matter.

"I'll go along with the scheme," Allie said with a sigh. "Only watch out for her mother."

When Jo arrived at the Nyes' home on Friday night for the scheduled sleepover, Taylor introduced Josephine to *both* of her mothers.

"Cin—rather, *Josephine*, this is Mother No. 1."

"So, you're Allie McAllister's daughter?" Mother No. 1 (aka Bobbie Nye) asked.

"Yes, Ms. Nye," Josephine answered respectfully.

"I taught your mother in high school. I suppose that you're another religious fanatic, like your mother before you."

"Not really. It's more my parents, actually."

"Good. There may be hope for you after all," Bobbie Nye said, unknowingly echoing her daughter's previous statement.

"And this is Mother No. 2," Taylor said.

"Pleased to meet you," Joyce Foster-Nye greeted her.

Unlike Bobbie, who always had been pleasantly plump but rather pretty, Joyce Foster was something of plain Jane, with wavy hair of a nondescript brown and gray eyes. Unlike her future daughter, Joyce had not been popular with the boys at school, and she had not experienced much romance in her life until Bobbie Nye had swept her off her feet during college, where they had been roommates.

Before they bedded down for the night, Taylor introduced her young friend to her love of horror movies. The Nyes let their daughter watch virtually anything, except religious movies, most of which had been banned by the government anyway. After the movie, it was time for bed. Josephine enjoyed her sleepover, and as promised, she didn't even try to witness to Taylor. In fact, as her parents had feared, Taylor was much more of a bad influence on their daughter than Jo was a good influence on Taylor.

CHAPTER 25

Josefiend

As much as the Holtzes wished that the sleepover was a one-time thing, sleeping over at her "best friend forever's" house became the constant request of their daughter. In order to counteract the potentially negative influence on their daughter's spiritual growth, Josephine's parents opened their home to Taylor as well. Jack and Allie would attempt to impart their Christian beliefs to the young pagan, but it was all for naught.

Little did they know that while the two girls pretended to listen, with intent looks upon their eager young faces, they later would hole up in Josephine's bedroom and giggle riotously over the preposterous theological tenets of Josephine's parents' antiquated religion. Josephine began to feel a thrill of mischievous pleasure at her burgeoning acts of teenage rebellion. But little by little, Josephine's behind-closed-doors disdain blossomed into out-in-the-open defiance.

The trouble began after Jo entered Our (First) Lady Hillary Rodham Clinton Middle School (or as the Holtzes sarcastically referred to it, Our *Almost* First Female President Hillary Rodham Clinton Middle School). If they had had their choice (which they didn't), they would have sent their only child anywhere but to this bastion of liberalism. Following seventh grade, however, during the summer of her thirteenth year, Josephine *really* began to rebel.

One Saturday afternoon in mid-July, Allie saw Josephine leaving the house and asked, "Where are you going?"

"Out," was Josephine's curt reply.

"Did you clean your room?" Allie asked.

"I'll do it later," Jo blithely promised as she opened the front door.

"No, you'll do it right now, young lady! You march your little derriere right back to your bedroom, and clean it up!"

"*You* clean it!" Josephine screamed at her.

"Don't you dare talk to your mother like that, Cindy Jo Holtz!"

"I'll talk to you anyway that I want to!" Cindy Jo answered defiantly, with her arms crossed. "And from now on, you will address me as Josephine."

That was the first time that Josephine revealed to either of her parents the name she'd been using for herself for some time.

"I'll address you as spoiled brat. Go to your room!" Allie ordered her.

Instead of going to her room, however, Josephine bolted out of the house (the Holtz family had upgraded from their apartment in Minneapolis to a modest two-bedroom house within the city limits). Jo returned hours later to find that her mother had cleaned her room for her—by throwing most of the contents of her room out of her bedroom window. The hostilities only intensified from there on.

Soon, Allie came up with the perfect sobriquet for the entity that had once been her dutiful daughter: Josefiend.

Mom and Dad Holtz were hardly pleased with this turn of events. Ever since their daughter had turned thirteen, she had also turned into a smart-mouthed teenage brat. Some of these unpleasant modifications were to be expected with the onset of normal adolescence, but this level of alteration was beyond the pale! And they couldn't help but wonder if a large part of the changes could be attributed to Josephine's unhealthy friendship with that Nye girl.

In a last-ditch effort to save their daughter's soul, not to mention their own sanity, the Holtzes put a stop to the sleepovers, but this was a fruitless gesture, since the two girls still saw each other at school five times a week. Jo also had easy access to Principal Nye at school, and she could drop by her office anytime and complain about the latest atrocity perpetrated by her "abusive" parents—like being forced to clean her room, do laundry, or generally help out around the house.

Unbeknownst to anyone other than Principal Nye and her daughter, Taylor, Taylor's befriending the Holtz girl had been instigated by Ms. Nye, who wanted to see if she could succeed with Allie's daughter where she had once failed with Allie—converting her to her liberal beliefs. So far, Bobbie Nye's scientific experiment was working far beyond her wildest expectations. She had successfully turned the daughter completely against her parents.

One day, Josephine came to Principal Nye's office and, after her usual torrent of complaints regarding her parents, confided to her, "I wish that you were my mother."

"There may be a way to make that wish come true," Ms. Nye confided conspiratorially.

One late afternoon in early October, at Billie Jo McAllister's not-so-modest house in the suburbs, Allie Holtz confided in her own mother over coffee. Mrs. McAllister was still slender and still had strawberry-blonde hair (with the occasional and most distressing gray hair creeping in), and she still worked as a certified public accountant.

Allie began the conversation by humbly admitting, "I realize that it's normal for teenagers to test parental boundaries, and I would imagine that I was quite a handful at that age—"

"You were an absolute angel," Mom McAllister countered. "It was your brother who was the devil incarnate."

"Thank you for the compliment, but we're really at our wit's end with Cindy Jo. Or Josephine, as she now insists on calling herself." Allie then elaborated on some of trials and tribulations that they were going through with their disobedient daughter. "I'm at the end of my rope here, Ma. I just don't know how much more of this I can take."

Then Allie broke down and wept. All of the months of frustration poured out of her, along with her tears. Allie's mother held her child close as Allie cried like a baby.

"It sounds like my granddaughter needs to be spanked good and proper," Grandmother Billie advised.

"If only we could," Allie moaned.

The progressive government had decreed that all forms of parental discipline constituted as child abuse, from spanking to grounding. Even parents raising their voices to their own children was now suspect. As a result, modern society was raising an entire generation of unruly, rebellious children, disobedient to even the most lax of parents.

Chapter 26

Not Turning the Other Cheek

Matters came to a head soon afterward. One Saturday evening in early October, Josephine (who was now thirteen years and four months old) exited her bedroom all decked out in an outfit in keeping with the current 1980s Goth revival—long black dress, torn black stockings, and black ankle-high laced boots. (Her parents later wondered *where* she'd gotten such attire. They had not bought it for her or sanctioned it.) She also was wearing a copious amount of makeup—white foundation, thick false eyelashes, black eye shadow, black lipstick, and black fingernail polish—and her red hair was dyed jet-black.

"Where are you going dressed like that?" her mother demanded.

Josephine gave her usual terse reply. "Out."

"Show some respect for your mother, young lady," Jack instructed his rude daughter.

"But how can I show respect for her if I don't possess any?" Josephine answered.

Resisting an urge to strike his disrespectful daughter right across her smart-aleck mouth, Jack instead interrogated her. "Your mother asked you a question: where are you going?"

"If you must know, I'm going out on a date—a double date, in fact."

"At your age? Absolutely not!" Mr. Holtz thundered.

"And not dressed like that," Mrs. Holtz added. "Do you honestly think that we would let you leave this house looking like a ghoul?"

"I'm not asking for your permission," Josephine said with a sneer. "I'm going out whether you like it or not!"

"Not if we lock you up in your bedroom," her father threatened.

"Then I'll just turn you both in for false imprisonment," Jo retorted.

"Please, Cin—er, Josephine," her mother pleaded. "We're only concerned about your welfare."

"It's only a date," Josephine argued. "Just dinner and a concert."

"Yeah? And I know just what this boy has in mind for dessert," Jack said, "assuming it's a boy we're discussing here and not some dirty old man."

"Or another girl," Allie added; she didn't know just how much the Nye family had rubbed off on their impressionable young daughter.

"Get your mind out of the gutter, you two," Josephine replied. "And I'll have you know that it is a boy. Taylor set me up with one of her boyfriend's friends."

"An older boy, I assume," Allie said.

"He's only a little bit older. Derek is sixteen—"

"Sixteen!" Mrs. Holtz gasped. "You're only thirteen!"

"I know how sixteen-year-old boys are. I was one once, you know," Jack said. "And at least I was a *Christian* boy, which I seriously doubt your date is."

"Don't worry about it. If something should happen this

evening, and I become pregnant as a result, I can always get an abortion," Josephine reasoned. "I don't need your permission to do that either."

Allie's immediate reaction to her daughter's provocative statement was to slap her hard across her impudent face. Far from turning the other cheek, Josephine ran for the safety of her bedroom, screaming, "You'll pay for that!" She spent the rest of the night in her bedroom while her parents pleaded with her to come out, and her mother begged for her forgiveness. (At least her parents didn't need to lock her up in her bedroom after all.)

When Josephine's proposed blind date arrived, along with his friend and Taylor Nye, it gave Mr. Holtz the utmost satisfaction to inform them all that the date was definitely off.

The next morning was Sunday, and the Holtzes' pouting daughter still refused to leave the safety of her bedroom. So her parents left her to go to church. The Holtz family did not attend a church in the traditional sense of the word, since the only Christian churches remaining were liberal mainline denominations, and no God-respecting Christian would ever darken their doors. Instead, the Holtzes, as well as the McAllisters, met at Ma McAllister's house, as the word *church* originally referred to the people, not the building, anyway.

The McAllister house church was more akin to a home Bible study or a prayer meeting than a formalized church service, and it consisted of reading passages from the Bible, followed by a discussion time, some corporate prayer, and the singing of a few hymns. This particular church was not recognized by the government, which meant that it enjoyed no tax-exempt status, but it endured no governmental interference either.

Josephine had only recently stopped attending the meetings, shortly after she had made her public declaration of disbelief. Rod and Cindy's daughter, Rose, however, was still content to remain in the faith. Though she was four years younger than her cousin Josephine, she was already as tall as her but not as slender. And she possessed the family traits of red hair and freckles.

The stress of the last week was etched upon the Holtzes' faces, particularly Allie's, from the moment that they first arrived.

Cindy took one look at them and asked, "What has my incorrigible namesake niece done to you now, Allie Cat?"

Jack and Allie relayed what had transpired the previous evening, and the gathered group prayed for the situation—mostly they prayed for Josephine's salvation. Following the weekly meeting of this peculiar *ecclesia*, the Holtzes drove back home. When they returned, Jack and Allie found that Josephine still refused to come out of her room (though they also found evidence that she had used their kitchen to break her longer-than-customary fast).

But even angry children need to eat (not to mention to use the restroom), so they knew that Josephine had to come up for air sooner or later. The Holtzes' intractable daughter finally surfaced around ten o'clock that night, after having skipped both Sunday lunch and dinner. Allie managed to catch Josephine between a much-needed restroom break and her raiding of the icebox, and Allie attempted once more to apologize to her.

"Jo, I'm sorry about what happened last night, but you really shouldn't speak so flippantly about murdering an innocent child."

"Meat is murder; abortion is a woman's constitutional right." Jo regurgitated what she had been taught at school.

"You can't seriously believe that!" Allie exclaimed.

"I don't know what I believe anymore," Josephine said softly.

She sounded so lost and confused (and so vulnerable) that Allie's heart couldn't help but go out to her, despite all of the recent conflict between them. She tried to use this opportunity to rebuild the dike.

"Whatever you're going through, we can face it together—you, your father, and I. And the Lord."

But then a wall suddenly seemed to come down inside her daughter's mind, a hardness returned to her cold gray eyes, and she answered in a voice that was as hard and as cold as the look in her eyes. "I don't believe in your Lord anymore—if I ever did. Apology not accepted!" With that, Josephine stormed back to her bedroom, taking with her whatever food she had managed to forage from the fridge. Once inside her room, she slammed and locked the door once more.

Allie, realizing that the moment had passed, slumped down into one of the kitchen chairs, lay her head down on the table, and wept. She couldn't help but think of Jesus Christ's words regarding the wicked one devouring the good seed that fell by the wayside like a bird. Or perhaps her daughter's heart was the stony ground on which the word fell. Whatever the case, Allie wondered how long her daughter could keep up this hostility toward her and how long she herself could stand this most unpleasant situation.

CHAPTER 27

Déjà Vu All Over Again

The next morning, Josephine stayed in her bedroom for as long as she dared before darting out of her room to make a mad dash for the school bus. Allie was thankful that her truculent daughter had opted to ride the bus; she didn't want to endure more of her daughter's silent treatment while driving her to school. As it was, Allie only caught a glimpse of her will-o'-the-wisp of a daughter as she flew out the door.

"Goodbye, Jo. I love you!" Allie called after her.

Allie didn't know if Jo had heard her or not, but she received no response. Then again, she hadn't really expected one.

Jo couldn't wait to tell Principal Nye what had transpired on Saturday night, but she had to wait until after calculus, her first-period class. At least that went by quickly enough, unimpeded by reciting the Pledge of Allegiance. School children were no longer required to stand up and pledge allegiance to the American flag with their hands over their hearts. There was no American flag to pledge allegiance to anymore. The globalists had gotten rid of all sectarian, nationalistic flags years ago.

The nation's flag and all progressive nations' flags had been replaced by the Global flag. The Global flag was a picture of the planet earth on a navy-blue background. Children were not obligated to pledge allegiance to this flag either. The teachers knew that the children's allegiance to the progressive government would be enforced by the police and the courts. The national anthem had also been abolished. Prior to that, so many sports players and citizens had refused to stand up for it at sporting events anyway.

Josephine's second period was free, so she skipped down to the principal's office and was given her usual preferential treatment. Principal Nye welcomed her warmly and asked if there was a reason for her visit. Josephine quickly forced some theatrical tears and dramatically said, "My mother slapped me!"

"Oh, my poor baby girl!" Ms. Nye sympathized as she came out from behind her desk. She crouched down to Josephine's height level and held her arms out to her.

Josephine ran into those waiting arms and cried, "My parents have been abusing me for years, and I just can't take it anymore!"

Principal Nye wasted little time in contacting the police, and the police also wasted little time in arresting the alleged perpetrators. Jack Holtz was easy enough to find; he was right under the police's noses, as he himself was a police officer. In Allie's case, a patrol car with two patrol officers was dispatched to the Holtz house. However, this time Allie was not taken in for questioning. Instead, the police read her the Miranda rights and placed her under arrest without interrogation.

Allie was taken to the Minneapolis police station, where she was fingerprinted. Her mug shot was taken, and she was strip-searched and outfitted in an orange jumpsuit, and then she was placed in a holding cell—it was déjà vu for her.

When Allie was granted her one phone call, she called her

brother, the lawyer, at home. Rod McAllister was out taking a deposition, but his wife, Cindy, answered the phone.

"Cindy?" Allie began tenuously.

Cindy could tell immediately that something was amiss with her best friend and sister-in-law. "Allie, what has Josephine done to you now?"

"She's had us arrested!" Allie exclaimed.

"Arrested? Not again! What are the charges?"

"Child abuse," Allie whispered into the phone. "I can't believe I was charged with such an offense!"

"Of all the ridiculous ... oh, yeah, that slap on the face," Cindy remembered.

"Yeah. I never should have lost my temper like that."

"You're only human. But it appears that your rebellious daughter is not going act divinely enough to forgive you for it. But did you say that she had both of you arrested?"

"Yes, she's accused both of us of child abuse."

"But Jack didn't slap her ... or did he?"

"No, but we have both administered spankings over the years, contrary to the laws of the land," Allie explained.

"Check. I'll inform your brother when he gets home of what transpired. And I'll tell your mother too. And of course, I'll be praying for you both."

"Thank you, Cin."

Rodney J. McAllister, attorney-at-law, managed to arrange bail for the accused (paid for by Billie Jo McAllister, certified public accountant, by taking out a second mortgage on her home), and he waived his usual fee out of fraternal affection (which wasn't saying much, since most of his work was done on a pro bono basis). A few days later, he met with his clients at his modest two-bedroom house in Darwin City to discuss the case.

"After much consideration, I have decided to not put either one of you on the witness stand."

"So we won't be allowed to defend ourselves against these heinous charges?" Jack asked.

"I fear the only result of your testifying would be to bury yourself, legally speaking. I doubt it would clear your names, and your honesty as Christians would force you to admit, under oath, that you've disciplined your daughter. And Allie would not only have to admit to administering corporal punishment on Josephine but also to slapping her—unless you're prepared to commit perjury, which is not only against civil law but, more importantly, against God's law."

"Thou shalt not bear false witness against thy neighbor," Jack said, quoting one of the Ten Commandments.

"I don't mind copping to that rash act of slapping Cindy Jo," Allie said, "but to be labeled as a child abuser alongside sadistic, psychopathic parents who really *do* abuse their children, all because I was performing my Christian duty as a parent, is ludicrous!"

"Well, ludicrous or not, child abuse is a very serious charge in these progressive times," Lawyer McAllister reminded his client and sister.

In child abuse cases, jury trials had long since been abrogated. Instead, the prosecution and defense lawyers would present their evidence (and witnesses) in front of a judge, and then the judge would deliberate and give his (or her) verdict.

As their trial date grew closer, the Holtzes were disappointed to learn that their case had not fallen on the Honorable Gloria Dawson's docket (the judge who had been so lenient with Allie the first time).

The presiding judge was to be the Honorable Daniel Simon. Judge Simon's first name translated as "judge of God" or "God is my judge" in the Hebrew tongue. In fact, Daniel Simon was a Jew by nationality, but he was far from a practicing Orthodox Jew, and he did not believe that God was his judge; he did not believe that God even existed in the first place. Judge Daniel was a short, spry, white-haired gentleman in his early sixties.

Lawyer McAllister's adversary was to be none other than Ms. Cherie Williams. Ms. Williams had been promoted to district attorney, which meant that she rarely tried cases herself, leaving that to her stable of assistant district attorneys. But DA Williams so relished a second chance to put Allison Holtz behind bars (along with her sanctimonious husband, as an added bonus) that she decided to forgo her usual privilege and to try the case herself.

Chapter 28

Fit to Be Tried

Much had changed in the dozen or so years since Allie's first trial and subsequent conviction (and most of it definitely not for the better). The left-wing progressives had gained substantial ground over the years; they had not only put a president in the White House, but they had also won both houses of Congress, and they owned most state and city officials as well. With such well-placed people, they were able to stack the Supreme Court (and most of the lower courts) with enough judicial activist judges to make their anti-Christian, globalist agenda the law of the land, oppressive though it was.

The Supreme Court had circumvented the Second Amendment of the United States Constitution by interpreting the "right to bear arms" clause as relating to only the police and the military. And while neither the courts nor the Congress could successfully outlaw Christianity (owing to that pesky prohibiting clause), they had succeeded in effectively neutering the Christians' ability to practice their religion through various laws that prohibited the free exercise of their faith, like sharing that faith with others.

Another tactic was to forbid parents from teaching any ideas that ran contrary to the teachings of the government-run schools (and virtually everything that was taught at those schools contradicted the tenets of Christianity) and from violating their children's personal autonomy by making them participate in any religious activities against their will. In that way, the government hoped to indoctrinate the succeeding generations of children until it ultimately eradicated biblical Christianity altogether.

The government's strict child-abuse laws also contributed to the hampering of Christian parents from raising their children in the "nurture and admonition of the Lord," which is how Jack and Allie Holtz, loving parents, found themselves in a court of law for the crime of child abuse. The accused arrived at the courthouse—ironically only a few yards from the police station where Jack worked. Or where he had previously worked; now he was on paid administrative leave, pending the outcome of his trial.

Etched in stone above the entrance of the courthouse was the motto of the progressive government:

Open Borders, Open Restrooms, Open Minds

Allie grimly remembered the parodies that her family had made up for the motto over the years: "Minds so open that they can't hold a conviction," or "So open that their brains fell out," and many others. But now the last laugh seemed to be on her and Jack.

Once inside the courtroom where the trial would take place, the defendants took their seats beside their lawyer at the defense table, and the State of Minnesota v. John and Allison Holtz trial began.

The prosecution gave her opening statement. "Your Honor, what we have before the court is as flagrant a case of child abuse as can be imagined. The perpetrators include a convicted felon who, after being let off with the proverbial slap on the wrist by your predecessor, Judge Dawson, repaid the state for its leniency by reoffending within a few short years following her conviction. The state will prove that John and Allison Holtz are not only horrible, abusive parents but that they are also a menace to progressive society. Thank you, Your Honor."

Then the defense took his turn. "Your Honor, the defense will prove that these trumped-up charges of child abuse against my clients—two of most loving parents that could possibly be found—are totally unfounded. Thank you, Your Honor."

The judge then instructed the prosecutor, "You may call your first witness."

"Thank you, Your Honor. The prosecution calls Ms. Bobbie Nye."

Principal Nye took the stand, wearing a sleeveless black dress. Bobbie Nye had been an idealistic biology teacher, fresh out of college and newly married, when she had fruitlessly attempted to convince a young Allie McAllister of the validity of evolution. Now she was around forty years old and was a respected principal. As she could have predicted roughly seventeen years ago, her former student had come to a decidedly bad end.

When asked by District Attorney Williams, Principal Nye began to relate what Josephine had told her about being abused.

"Objection, Your Honor. Hearsay evidence," Rod said.

"Sustained," Judge Simon said. "The witness will please confine her testimony to what she herself has observed."

District Attorney Williams then changed her tactics.

"Principal Nye, did you ever observe any physical evidence of the abuse?"

"Not actually," Principal Nye answered truthfully, "but I would say that I had observed negative psychological effects of child abuse in young Ms. Josephine Holtz."

"No further questions, Your Honor," DA Williams said.

"Your witness," Judge Simon instructed Rod.

"Thank you, Your Honor. Ms. Nye, you testified that you observed negative psychological effects of child abuse in Josephine Holtz."

"Yes," Bobbie answered curtly; she was openly antagonist toward the defense lawyer. She didn't care for most men but Christian men in particular.

"Do you hold a degree in psychology?" Rod asked.

"No, but—"

"No further questions, Your Honor," Lawyer McAllister abruptly said.

"Would the prosecution like to redirect this witness?" Judge Simon asked.

"Yes, Your Honor," DA Williams answered. "Principal Nye, keeping in mind that you are not a psychologist, have you been properly trained in how to recognize the effects of bullying or child abuse in a student?"

"Yes, I have," Ms. Nye stated proudly.

Allie couldn't help remembering how her complaints had fallen on deaf ears whenever she'd complained to the administrators at Open Minds Elementary School and Hillary Clinton Middle School (and to Principal Nye herself) regarding the constant bullying that her daughter had endured for years until Josephine and Taylor had become bosom buddies. Obviously, Ms. Nye's facility did not extend to her spotting bullying if it was perpetrated by her favored daughter, Taylor.

"In your professional opinion," Ms. Williams continued, "did you observe any signs of child abuse in the victim?"

"Objection. Calls for speculation on the part of the witness," Mr. McAllister contended.

"Not in my opinion; objection overruled. The witness will please answer the question," Judge Simon instructed.

"Yes, I did observe several signs of abuse," Principal Nye answered.

"Could you please elaborate?" DA Williams requested.

"Objection. Counsel is leading the witness," Mr. McAllister interrupted.

"Once again, not in my opinion; objection overruled," Judge Simon repeated. "The witness will please answer the question."

"Yes, Your Honor," Ms. Nye said. "Josephine was withdrawn. She lacked self-esteem. She often expressed a reluctance to go home at the end of the school day. She even exhibited physical manifestations, like headaches and stomachaches."

It was true that Josephine was, by nature, introverted (or at least, she had been introverted until she'd become a loud-mouthed teenaged brat as of late), but it was school where she had once feared to go, even complaining of physical ailments in an attempt to stay home (once again, until she developed her friendship with her former chief tormentor, Taylor).

"No further questions, Your Honor," Ms. Williams said.

"The witness may step down," Judge Simon instructed. "Court is adjourned until tomorrow morning at nine o'clock."

Chapter 29

Grand Perjury

The next day, District Attorney Williams called Principal Nye's unnaturally conceived daughter to the stand. As Taylor Nye's tall, slender body (dressed in a long, white silk dress) bounded up to the witness stand and flopped down on the chair, it was obvious that the recently turned fourteen-year-old girl relished being the center of attention. Young Ms. Nye was sworn in, and DA Williams began to question her (whereupon Taylor gleefully lied through her braces-covered teeth).

"Now, Ms. Nye, are you friends with Josephine Holtz?"

"Oh yes, Ms. Williams. Josephine and I are best friends."

"And you have spent much time over at the Holtzes' home?"

"Yes, I have slept over there bunches of times."

"And in all of that time, did you ever observe any evidence of the abuse that the Holtzes inflicted on Josephine?"

"Yes, I have, Ms. Williams."

"Could you please elaborate?" District Attorney Williams requested.

"Objection. Counsel is leading the witness," Mr. McAllister interrupted.

"Once again, not in my opinion. Objection overruled. The witness will please answer the question," Judge Simon said.

"Well, Josephine was always telling me about how her parents would—"

"Objection, Your Honor. Hearsay evidence," Lawyer McAllister said.

"Sustained," Judge Simon ruled. "This witness will also confine her testimony to what she has actually observed."

"Yes, Your Honor," Taylor answered. She seemed to contemplate for a moment and then said, "Well, one time when I was over at Josephine's house, and we were goofing around in her bedroom, Mrs. Holtz stuck her head in the doorway and told Josephine to stop all the nonsense immediately. I personally think that Josephine's mother just couldn't stand the thought of her daughter have any fun."

"Objection, Your Honor. The witness is purporting to know what my client was thinking," Rod said.

"Sustained. The witness will once again confine her testimony—"

"Sorry, Your Honor," Taylor interrupted. "Anyway, Mrs. Holtz told Jo that she had to work on her scripture memorization. Jo's parents were always having her—"

"Objection, Your Honor. The witness is generalizing," Rod said.

"Sustained; the witness will please stick to the facts," Judge Simon ordered.

"Yes, Your Honor," Taylor repeated, but this time her voice displayed annoyance at these constant interruptions and restrictions. "Josephine's mother told her that she had to memorize an entire chapter of the Bible before bedtime, and when Jo made the mistake of saying 'in a minute' before she complied with the order, her mother hauled off and smacked her right across the mouth!"

The spectators in the gallery gasped and murmured until Judge Simon gaveled them into silence.

Allie was becoming more and more incensed. She'd never forced her daughter to memorize scripture, and she and Jack had never required Josephine to memorize entire chapters at one stretch either. And she'd only slapped her daughter that *one* time, on the night of Josephine's aborted first date.

"Please continue, Ms. Nye," Ms. Williams requested.

"Thank you, Ms. Williams. Anyway, Mrs. Holtz slapped Jo's face and hissed, 'That's for talking back to your mother!' Then she violently pulled Jo off of her bed by her arm and began spanking her right in front of me and—"

Allie couldn't take it anymore. She jumped up and exclaimed, "Lies! All lies!"

"Counselor, please instruct your client to afford this court the proper respect, or I shall be forced to hold the defendant in contempt of court," Judge Simon warned.

"Yes, Your Honor," Rod McAllister said. Then he whispered to his client, "Sit down and shut up, Al. You're not helping your case."

Allie did as she was told, fuming all the while. She hadn't spanked Josephine since Jo was ten years old, and she had certainly never had spanked her in front of Taylor.

"The witness will please continue," Judge Simon instructed.

"Yes, Your Honor. Then Jo's mother dragged her into the living room, while threatening her. She said, 'Stop crying, or I'll really give you something to cry about!' I was shocked. Neither one of my mothers has ever treated me like that."

"No further questions, Your Honor," DA Williams said.

"Your witness, Mr. McAllister," Judge Simon instructed.

"Thank you, Your Honor," Mr. McAllister acknowledged. "So, Miss Nye, you testified earlier that you and Miss Josephine Holtz are best friends."

"That's correct," Taylor answered with mock pleasantness.

"Obviously, you must be referring to more recent times, after you'd spent years bullying her because of her Christian faith."

"Objection, Your Honor. Relevancy," Ms. Williams said.

"Sustained," Judge Simon ruled. "The witness will disregard the question."

"Keeping in mind that you are under oath, Miss Nye, are you being completely honest regarding the incident that you've just relayed?" Rod asked.

"Objection, Your Honor. Counsel is impugning my witness' honesty."

"Overruled. The witness will please answer the question—honestly."

"As Darwin is my witness, I am being completely and totally honest," Taylor said.

"Charles Darwin has been dead for centuries. And since our public schools teach that there is no eternal life, then how could Darwin be your witness?" Rod asked.

"Your Honor, Mr. McAllister is making a mockery of these proceedings!"

"Sustained. The witness will refrain from answering the question. Watch yourself, Mr. McAllister, or I'll hold *you* in contempt of court!" Judge Simon threatened.

"No further questions, Your Honor," Mr. McAllister said, concluding his cross-examination.

"Would the prosecution like to redirect this witness?" Judge Simon asked.

"No, thank you, Your Honor," Ms. Williams answered.

"The witness may step down," Judge Simon instructed. "Call your next witness."

"The state calls Ms. Cynthia Josephine Holtz," DA Williams announced.

Chapter 30

Bearing False Witness

Ms. Cynthia Josephine Holtz took the stand, dressed much more conservatively than she had been on the night of her proposed double date. She was wearing a calf-length pink dress and a cute pair of white boots that were functional for the Midwest winter in which Minnesota was currently held captive. Josephine's mother had often been mistaken for being younger than she was, but Josephine, at four foot eleven and ninety pounds, looked closer to ten years old than her actual thirteen years.

Josephine wore braces on her teeth like her best friend, Taylor, but she was not as pretty as Taylor, and her thin face and high cheekbones gave her a continually gaunt look. Josephine's immature-looking frame and delicate features made her appear even more like the helpless child-abuse victim that the prosecution was purporting her to be. After she was sworn in, District Attorney Williams began her direct examination.

"Ms. Holtz, could you please describe, in your own words, your relationship with your parents?"

"Primarily, my relationship with my parents was one based on fear—fear of what they would do to me if I dared to disobey or neglected to obey any of the thousands of rules that they placed upon me."

Any hope that Josephine's parents had that their rebellious daughter would come to her senses, repent of her waywardness, and resubmit herself to her parents' authority were dashed by Josephine's opening statement.

"Objection, Your Honor," Josephine's uncle Rodney said. "This witness is exaggerating."

"Sustained. The witness will please confine her testimony to the facts."

"Yes, Your Honor," DA Williams acknowledged. "Please continue, Ms. Holtz."

"Yes, Ms. Williams. My parents had a multitude of rules for me to follow regarding how I interacted with teachers and fellow students. Would word *multitude* be considered an exaggeration, Your Honor?" Josephine asked meekly.

"I think that *multitude* would be acceptable," Judge Simon decided. "Pray continue, Ms. Holtz."

"I tried to be a good girl. I tried to pray without ceasing, no matter how much my knees ached—I spent hours on end kneeling in front of my bed. I tried to keep up with the chapters of daily Bible reading and scripture memorization, in addition to keeping up with my mounting schoolwork."

Obviously, Jack and Allie had encouraged their daughter to pray, to read her Bible, and to memorize scripture passages, but they never forced her to do it, particularly not after she had apostated.

"And what would happen to you if you failed to obey any these rules?" District Attorney Williams inquired.

"My parents would"—Josephine dramatically bit her quivering lip—"they would *spank* me!" Josephine broke down and wept, as the spectators once again murmured among themselves.

"Order in the court!" Judge Simon said.

Once Josephine had composed herself, Ms. Williams once again requested that she continue.

"Yes, Ms. Williams. I tried to be a good daughter. I did! But sooner or later, I would fail, and then would come the inevitable punishment."

"Who would administer these spankings?" Ms. Williams asked.

"Usually, it was my mother, since Dad was often at work."

"Ms. Holtz, could you please describe, in your own words, what occurred on the evening of last October 10?"

"Yes, Ms. Williams. All I wanted to do was to go out on a date, to have a little bit of enjoyment in my life, but my parents objected, of course. My father ordered me to go to my room, and when I tried to reason with them, my mother slapped me!"

At this admission, more whispering and gavel banging occurred.

"No further questions, Your Honor," Ms. Williams concluded.

"Court is recessed for one hour," Judge Simon announced.

Following the lunch recess, Rod McAllister cross-examined his niece.

"Now, Miss Holtz, do you mean to tell this court that your parents actually forced you to pray and to read your Bible?"

"Well, they didn't have to force me to do it at first. But after I stopped believing in my parents' foolish religion, I wanted to stop doing what I knew to be a waste of time, but they wouldn't let me!"

Defense Attorney McAllister paused for a moment before

he looked straight into his niece's eyes and asked her point-blank, "Cynthia Josephine, are you being completely honest with this court? And remember that you are under oath."

"Objection, Your Honor. Counsel is badgering this witness," Williams contended.

"Overruled; the witness will please answer the question," Judge Simon decreed.

Josephine bit her lip and looked away. Allie fervently prayed that her daughter would finally do the right thing and put an end to this continuing nightmare. But when Jo's head turned back toward her parents, she had that cold look in her eyes again, the same one she'd displayed that Sunday night in October following their altercation.

Then she looked right into her mother's eyes and calmly intoned, "I am being completely and absolutely honest—so help me God."

Allie's heart broke. It was bad enough that her precious daughter was lying under oath, but to invoke the name of God (obviously just to spite her mother and father) was pure evil. Without realizing it, Josephine was inviting God's judgment upon her if she did not someday repent.

Josephine's uncle looked askance at his blaspheming, hard-hearted niece and then he sighed in abject defeat. "No further questions, Your Honor."

"Does the prosecution wish to redirect this witness?" Judge Simon asked Ms. Williams.

District Attorney Williams smiled triumphantly and replied, "No need to, Your Honor. The prosecution rests."

"Court is adjourned until nine tomorrow morning," Judge Simon announced.

Chapter 31

Defenseless

Defense Attorney Rodney J. McAllister started to present his case the next day, but his decision not to put his clients on the stand did not leave him with much material to mount a proper defense. Since he had also decided not to put his and Allie's mother on the stand for much the same reasons, Rod called Dr. Laura Ward as his first witness. Dr. Ward, dressed in a conservative navy-blue blouse and skirt, was still big and tall and still rather attractive, even though she now past forty years old.

Dr. Ward had changed more inwardly than outwardly in the nearly fourteen years that had elapsed since she'd once counseled Allie to abort her child. Laura Ward had been a young doctor, just out of residency, when she'd become the McAllister family physician, one who firmly believed a woman should have a fulfilling career before she even considered giving birth, and that a responsible doctor should advise an abortion to any woman who was under twenty-five years of age.

But over the years, after observing the way that Allie Holtz had nurtured her only daughter, Dr. Ward began to suspect that what she had been taught in medical school was false. Eventually, she began conversing with Mrs. Holtz regarding her strange faith, and Allie, risking another charge of proselytizing, led her to the Lord. Obviously, Laura Ward's conversion led her to change her views on abortion. And she would've counseled expectant mothers against abortion, if the government would have left her that option.

A few years after Josephine's birth, the US Secretary of Population Control decreed that all women in the United States of America (aka the Progressive States of America) be limited to one child only, in accordance with the dictates of the other progressively minded countries in the European-American Union. Any female who became pregnant a second time was forced to undergo a government-paid-for abortion, and sterilization was ordered after the third offense.

Dr. Laura Ward took the witness stand, and Defense Attorney McAllister began questioning her.

"Dr. Ward, you are the family physician of the Holtz family?"

"Yes, I am, ever since Allison Holtz was eighteen years old."

"So in that capacity, you have given Miss Cynthia Josephine Holtz several physicals over the years?"

"At least one per year over the past thirteen-plus years," Dr. Ward confirmed.

"And have you at any time ever observed any signs of physical abuse on Miss Josephine Holtz?"

"None whatsoever," Dr. Ward answered with confidence.

"No further questions, Your Honor," Rod concluded.

"Your witness, Madam Prosecutor," Judge Simon instructed.

"Thank you, Your Honor. Dr. Ward, is it not true that physical abuse, such as the type that would be caused by corporal punishment, would be virtually impossible to detect, unless the victim is examined immediately afterward?"

"That is correct," Dr. Ward admitted. "Obviously, if the

abuse was extensive enough to cause permanent physical damage to the patient, then the effects would still be evident. But for the normal parental disciplining of the child—"

"There is no 'normal' disciplining of a child, either physical or emotional; it is all unconscionable, and it is all against the law! That is why we are holding this trial in the first place!" District Attorney Williams reminded the witness. Then she more calmly said, "One more question, Dr. Ward, you stated in your medical records that you originally advised Mrs. Holtz to abort her child. Is that correct?"

"Yes," Dr. Ward conceded, "but I wouldn't give such advice today."

"One is left to wonder if poor Josephine would've been better off if Allison Holtz had heeded that advice," Ms. Williams mused. "No further questions, Your Honor."

The district attorney turned on her heel and walked back to the prosecution table.

"Does the defense wish to redirect this witness?" Judge Simon asked Rod.

"Yes, Your Honor. Dr. Ward, much like Principal Nye, have you been trained to spot the negative emotional effects of child abuse in children?"

"Yes, I have," Dr. Ward answered.

"Have you ever observed anything in Miss Holtz's behavior that would lead you to believe that she had been abused, either physically or emotionally?"

"No, I have not, Mr. McAllister," Dr. Ward stated for the record.

"No further questions, Your Honor."

"Call your next witness, Counselor," Judge Simon directed.

"Thank you, Your Honor. The defense calls Dr. Cynthia McAllister."

"Objection, Your Honor!" DA Williams said. "A defense attorney calling his own spouse as a material witness is not only highly irregular, but it is also exceedingly suspect! It's bad enough that the defense attorney is the brother and brother-in-law of the defendants, but this is going too far! Besides, her field is in drug rehabilitation, not—"

"Your Honor," Rod argued, "Dr. McAllister, though admittedly not a child psychologist, is being called due to her expertise in the field of psychology, in order to refute the testimony of Principal Nye, who has freely admitted that she herself is not a psychologist, regardless of Dr. McAllister's marital status."

Judge Simon paused briefly before he replied. "The court is recessed so that I can contemplate the implications of allowing such testimony."

The recess lasted for about thirty minutes. Once the trial resumed, Judge Simon reentered the courtroom, sat down, and gave his ruling. "Objection sustained. This court feels that the matrimonial relationship between this proposed witness and the defense attorney, not to mention her friendship with the defendants, would constitute such undue bias as to render her professional testimony both null and void. Dr. McAllister could, of course, be used as a character witness, as a friend of the accused, but not in her capacity as a trained psychologist."

After weighing what little benefit his wife's nonprofessional testimony would accomplish, a defeated Rodney McAllister sighed. "The defense rests."

"Court is adjourned until nine o'clock Monday morning, at

CHAPTER 32

Arguments and Apologies

The prosecution began their closing arguments the next Monday morning.

"Your Honor, the state has proven beyond the shadow of a doubt that the accused taught their innocent daughter fanciful myths contrary to the irrefutable truths imparted in our public schools by qualified instructors, and they compounded their crimes against the state by sadistically abusing their poor daughter for years on end. If I were a congresswoman, I would propose legislation to sterilize religious fanatics like Allison Holtz before they can give birth to even one child!

"But I am not a congresswoman; I am the duly appointed district attorney for the county of Hennepin. And as the county's representative, my job is to see that criminals like the Holtzes are put behind bars for the good of society. I humbly request, Honorable Judge Simon, that you do not make the same mistake that your predecessor made and that you show no mercy to malefactors like John and Allison Holtz. Thank you, Your Honor."

The defense's closing argument followed. "Your Honor, District Attorney Williams's comments plainly show why my clients had no hope of a fair trial in this county, considering the current political climate. The fact is, the only evidence the state presented was that of two disobedient children who have been so corrupted by our public school system that they shamelessly lied under oath without the slightest qualms and without any pang of guilt.

"The truth is that my clients love their daughter; they love her enough to correct her faults and to raise her to be a responsible citizen, actions which your legislators, Ms. Williams, have made a crime! Aside from one intemperate act on the part of Mrs. Holtz, my clients have done nothing wrong, and any society that says differently is the real criminal here. I ask you, Your Honor, to take this into consideration, and I ask for leniency for my clients. Thank you, Your Honor."

Last was District Attorney Cherie Williams's rebuttal. "Leniency? The last time that this lawbreaker Allison Holtz was tried, the judge showed her leniency, and look at the result: a young girl, Josephine Holtz, who will most probably be scarred for life as a result of the abuse that she suffered at her cruel parents' hands. Nay, I say no mercy for these criminals! The Holtzes are unfit to be parents; they are unfit to walk free among us in society; they are unfit to live! I demand that they be found guilty and be incarcerated to the full extent of the law! Thank you, Your Honor."

"The court is adjourned for the day," the Honorable Daniel Simon announced. "The attorneys will be informed when I've made my decision."

Judge Simon reconvened court the next morning. The interested parties and interested spectators arrived and were seated. The defendants were instructed to rise, and then the judge gave his ruling.

"There appears to be ample evidence to support the state's claim that the defendants, John and Allison Holtz, are guilty of teaching their child information that is contrary to young Ms. Josephine Holtz's public school education and that they are also guilty of an even more egregious offense—they are guilty of physically and emotionally abusing their daughter, as child abuse has been defined by both national and state law.

"Mr. Holtz has served both his country and this city with distinction in his roles of both soldier and police officer. But that service does not counteract the crimes that he has perpetrated upon his innocent daughter. Nobody is above the law, especially someone who has sworn to uphold that law. Thus, this court finds John David Holtz and Allison Jane McAllister Holtz guilty of child abuse and of contributing to the miseducation of a minor. A sentencing hearing is scheduled for April 1. Court is adjourned."

The sentencing hearing took place roughly a week later on the morning of April 1. After Judge Simon had the Holtzes rise, he asked, "Would the convicted like to address the court before I pass judgment on them?"

"Yes, Your Honor," Jack answered. "I guess this is the time when I'm supposed to throw myself on the mercy of the court and say that I'm sorry for what I've done. But how can I apologize for doing what I know to be right? Scripture states, 'He that spareth the rod hateth his son,' and 'Foolishness is bound in the heart of a child; but the rod of correction shall drive it far from him.' Thus, I will not apologize for my actions.

"However, I do plead for leniency on behalf of my darling wife, Allison. As the head of the household, the duty for training up my child in the way that she should go is primarily my responsibility. Please don't make my wife suffer for simply honoring my headship in this matter. Thank you, Your Honor."

Then Jack's darling wife, Allison, spoke. "I agree with what my husband has said, Your Honor, except that I feel that I should share in whatever punishment you impose upon him. In fact, if blame is to be meted out, then I deserve most of it since it was my rash act that set in motion the wheels of justice, which are no doubt poised to grind us both to powder. But I would like to address my daughter, if I may, since this might be the last chance that I will be able to speak to her, at least for some time."

"I will allow you this, Mrs. Holtz," Judge Simon said magnanimously.

Allie turned toward her daughter and quietly spoke.

"Cindy Jo, I apologize for slapping you like I did, and I apologize for being far from the best of mothers, but I don't apologize for doing my duty as a Christian parent. Cynthia Josephine, you know that you have lied to this court, and more important, you have lied before God. Your father and I both forgive you for this, and we still love you. I pray that you will someday seek God's forgiveness for your sins as well."

Allie thought that her daughter's face, which had been inscrutable throughout much of the trial, had just undergone some change. Josephine whispered something to the prosecutor, and then Ms. Williams stood up and informed the judge, "Your Honor, before you pass sentencing, Ms. Holtz would like to speak to you."

"Does the young Ms. Holtz wish to address the court?"

"Actually, she wishes to speak to you privately," Ms. Williams clarified.

"Very well. Ms. Holtz may speak to me in my chambers. This court will take a half-hour recess," Judge Simon announced.

CHAPTER 33

Stuck in Prairie Prison

The judge, the prosecutor, and the star witness exited the courtroom for Judge Simon's chambers. Once they departed, Jack whispered to his wife, "I think that your speech may have finally gotten to our deceitful daughter."

"I sure hope so," Allie said. "Maybe she finally will tell the truth."

"I hope so too," Rod answered, "because I'm afraid that I have failed you both."

"You did the best you could under the circumstances," Allie encouraged him.

"We probably never had a chance in this always-believe-the-victim climate," Jack agreed.

Once the conference in the chambers ended and the participating individuals returned to their seats, Judge Simon declared, "Mr. and Mrs. Holtz, I was inclined to throw the book at both of you for the unconscionable way you have treated your own daughter. But you should be thankful to the deity that you so foolishly believe in that your daughter still loves you—loves you enough to beg for clemency on your behalf. Your remarkable young daughter has just proposed a most ingenious solution; namely, that I grant both of you probation in exchange for my declaring her an emancipated teen.

"However, I feel that I would be remiss in my duties if I was to let Mrs. Allison Holtz off with only probation a second time. This would imply that a malefactor can offend against the laws of this state with impunity! And I would be loath to have Mrs. Holtz think that she can keep getting off scot-free. Thus, I'm about to make a judgment worthy of that mythical figure with which I'm sure the Holtzes are familiar: King Solomon.

"Since this is his first offense, I am ordering a five-year probation for Mr. John David Holtz. However, since this is Mrs. Allison Jane Holtz's second offense, and she appears to have been the main disciplinarian of the family, I am ordering six months incarceration at the minimum-security political prison located in Prairie, Minnesota, to be followed by an additional five-year probation once her prison term is completed.

"Conditions for the parole are as follows: Mr. and Mrs. Holtz will have absolutely no contact whatsoever with their daughter, unless young Ms. Holtz initiates said contact. In addition, besides observing the current ban on bearing any other children, the Holtzes, having been found guilty of child abuse and, by extension, found to be unfit parents, are not allowed to adopt children, run a day care, babysit, or have any contact with any persons under the legal age of fifteen, even including any of their underage relatives.

"Furthermore, the Holtzes will be required to undergo sensitivity counseling, as conducted by a licensed therapist employed by the state, for the entire length of their probation, in the hope that they may learn how to treat others, particularly children, with tolerance. And last, I have also decided to grant Ms. Holtz's petition for emancipation. Naturally, at the age of thirteen, Ms. Cynthia Josephine Holtz will not possess all of the rights and privileges pertaining to adulthood, but she is legally declared emancipated from her abusive parents from this day forward. Court is now adjourned."

"So much for making an impression on Josefiend," Allie whispered.

But it was only a momentary display of gallows humor before she burst into tears at the very thought of her upcoming prison sentence. Six months in prison might as well have been an eternity. Allie and her family were devastated. Though it was only a minimum security political prison, it was a prison sentence nevertheless. Allie barely had time to kiss her husband goodbye before she was hauled off to jail.

Prairie Prison was located in the town formally known as Eden Prairie. The reformatory was reserved for political dissidents, mostly Christians who had run afoul of the progressive government. In a sense, the state had put all of its rotten eggs in one basket (a "basket of deplorables," to borrow the phrase from former First Lady and failed presidential candidate Hillary Clinton). Allie began her six-month prison sentence there on April 1. It seemed like a cruel April Fool's Day joke had been played upon her.

Allie entered the prison with much fear and trembling; she had heard how even hardened criminals treated child abusers. And while their ire was mostly reserved for child sexual abusers, she wasn't sure if they would make that distinction in her particular case. But she also knew that "all things work together for good to them that love God, to them who are called according to His purpose." She had to trust in that and in her Lord.

Once Allie had arrived at Prairie Prison, she was stripped, deloused, and dressed in an orange jumpsuit, which matched her hair color but did absolutely nothing for her figure. Then she was conducted to her assigned cell. Once the cell door was ominously slammed shut, Allie wearily collapsed onto the bunk that had been graciously provided for her by the state of Minnesota and cried like a baby. Now the reality of her hopeless plight came down upon her like a proverbial ton of bricks.

Once she was all cried out (for now, at least), Allie sat up and tried to calmly assess the situation. She was certainly not the first person to have been jailed unjustly: Joseph in Egypt, Jeremiah, the apostle Paul, and Peter, and virtually all of the first-century disciples, eventually. They were all innocent too; even her Lord Jesus Christ had been falsely accused and convicted. This information didn't exactly cause her to sing praises out loud to God, as had Paul and Silas in Ephesus, but it did comfort her some.

At first, Allie was pleasantly surprised to discover that she had her cell all to herself. But then she figured that she must be between cellmates and that it was only a temporary situation. And she was right; the next day she was joined in her lonely prison cell by another woman. The new arrival was shorter and looked a little younger than she. She had black hair, ebony eyes, and an olive complexion. In the spirit of Christian friendship, Allie introduced herself.

"Hi. I'm Allie."

"Maria," the newcomer replied guardedly. She sat down on the other bunk, and asked Allie, "What are you in for?"

"Well, actually, the charge was child abuse." Maria eyed her cellmate suspiciously until Allie added, "And teaching my child information contrary to the teachings of public school."

34

I've Been Working on the (Underground) Railroad

In time (as they were doing time), Allie learned much about her cellmate. Maria Delgado was of Hispanic descent and was, as many Hispanics are, an adherent of the Roman Catholic religion. The Roman Catholic Church still existed, and it was (as it always had been) more concerned with political advancement than in advancing Jesus Christ's kingdom on earth (particularly the Roman Catholic hierarchy), but many of the rank-and-file Roman Catholic laypeople genuinely attempted to live out their faith.

In order to get on with the progressive world governments, the current pope had capitulated on many moral issues (climate change, gay and transgender rights, etc.). However, the latest Pope John Paul would not budge on the issue of abortion. Reasoning that contraceptives (as long as they weren't abortifacient) were the lesser of two evils (the other evil being abortion), the Holy Father allowed members of the Holy Mother church to use birth-control techniques in addition to the rhythm method for the first time in history.

These methods, however, were hardly foolproof, and they did not always prevent conception. Even as powerful a person as the current pope pled in vain with the progressive governments of the world—and most governments of the world were now progressive, other than the rulers of the Islamic countries—to at least allow the option of adoption in these cases. But adoption wouldn't solve the problem of overpopulation, the progressive powers that be argued.

Thanks to the open-borders policy of the progressive governments of Europe and of the United States, which allowed refugees and illegal aliens to flood into the West (which meant more mouths to feed and fewer jobs to go around to feed them), not to mention Obamacare virtually bankrupting the United States' economy, these socialistic policies had brought their respective countries to the brink of disaster. Abortion was now seen by the progressive leaders as the only way to stem the tide of eventual financial ruin.

Thus, any female who conceived a child a second time was ordered to undergo an abortion for the good of society. But many women (not only Roman Catholics but also Christians, Mormons, Muslims, and even nonreligious women who happened to possess a conscience) refused to submit to aborting their second child (or any subsequent children, for that matter). For those women who couldn't bring themselves to snuff out the lives of their innocent unborn children there arose an illegal option.

An underground railroad had been established to hide expectant mothers (and the resulting children) from the power of the progressive governments of the world. Maria Delgado ran one the relay stations for the underground railroad. Her involvement with this subversive activity was eventually discovered by the authorities; she was then arrested, tried, and convicted of sedition. As a result, she was summarily ripped away from her husband and her only son and incarcerated at Prairie Prison.

Allie and Maria soon put aside their theological differences and often prayed together and eventually read the Bible together. One of the precious few amenities that the prisoners had was the privilege (not the right) of a single copy of the Holy Bible located in the prison library. This concession had been hard fought, before the liberals (who had argued that the holy scriptures would only fan the flame of Christian sedition) took pity upon the poor incarcerated souls and finally granted their petition.

Obviously, given that most of the prisoners of Prairie Prison were religious, that lone Bible was a hot commodity. Prisoners had to go on a waiting list before they could come into temporary possession of the much-sought-after item. Once their time at bat came, they were allowed to possess this prize for only one week. Since the two cellmates were both new arrivals, their place in this process was smack-dab at the end of the line.

While they waited, they continued to pray together. Maria always prayed the Our Father and Hail Mary prayers that she'd learned by rote as a child. But Allie's prayers were radically different; she prayed as if she intimately knew to whom she was praying.

One day after Allie had finished praying, Maria asked her, "How did you learn to pray like that?"

"I've always prayed like this—or at least I have ever since I was saved."

"Saved? Saved from what?"

"You know, saved from the penalty of sin; saved from hell."

"Only by keeping the sacraments can we escape hell. And even then, everyone must spend years and years in purgatory—other than the holy saints, that is."

"Anyone who has accepted Jesus Christ as their personal Savior *is* a saint. Besides, purgatory doesn't exist. A disembodied soul either goes to heaven or to hell."

"I refuse to listen to this heresy anymore!" Maria exclaimed as she clapped her hands over her ears. Then she turned her back on Allie, grabbed her rosary, and started fervently reciting the Hail Mary.

This exchange caused a rift between the two cellmates that lasted for a number of days. Mrs. Holtz regretted her botched attempt at witnessing to her new friend, and she was aggrieved by the resulting distance between them that it had caused.

Allie went on with her prison life, eating in the mess hall, whiling her time away in the yard, praying to God in her cell, and waiting for her time with the public Holy Bible. This was interspersed with limited contact with family and friends. Regrettably, this contact was accomplished via a telephone and was conducted through a thick pane of bulletproof glass, which prevented any physical contact with her visitors, which was especially hard on Allie whenever her husband visited.

But Allie was thankful for the little time that she had with Jack, who visited her as much as possible, even though she was susceptible to a profound melancholy whenever the visit was over, and she returned to her lonely prison cell. At first, Jack had much time on his hands to visit his wife—he had lost his job with the police department, as it wouldn't do to have a convicted child abuser on the force.

But then Jack informed Allie, one day during a visit, "Well, I finally found a job."

"Thank God," Allie cheered. "Where are you working now?"

"I've been hired as a security guard at a church. Obviously, my new employers and I have agreed to disagree on matters of theology, but hiring a convicted criminal on probation appealed to their charitable inclinations. The pay is nowhere as good as I was making before, but it sure beats going on welfare. So how are you holding up?"

Allie sighed. "I'm doing as well as can be expected under the present circumstances—except that I've had something of a falling out with my cellmate."

"What's the problem?" Jack asked.

"Theological differences in my case too. My cellmate, Maria Delgado, is a Roman Catholic—"

"Say no more" Jack interrupted. "Though some Roman Catholics are closer to the truth than many a liberal mainline Protestant Church congregant is these days."

"Anyway, please pray for her that she will 'come unto the knowledge of the truth.' And pray for me as well."

"That you 'may open your mouth boldly, to make known the mystery of the gospel'?" Jack quoted. "I have never ceased praying for you, my love. But speaking of praying, let me pray for you right now. Father, I ask you to watch over my beloved wife and to protect her. Give her boldness to share her faith and wisdom to know when and how to share it. Make her 'wise as a serpent and harmless as a dove.' And I pray that Maria Delgado may realize her need for God's forgiveness, which is only found through faith in Jesus Christ, Your Son. Amen."

After the spouses prayed together via the telephone link-up,

Jack departed, as visiting hours were over. Allie went back to her cell, feeling a mixture of sadness at being parted from her husband again and the spiritual empowerment she always felt whenever her godly husband prayed for her.

CHAPTER 35

Emancipation Proclamation

O n the outside, things were going significantly better for Allie's emancipated teen daughter. Obviously, at age thirteen, Josephine's emancipation was much truer in theory than in practice. She was still a couple of months shy of fourteen years old, the age required for obtaining her driver's license, and over a year away from the legal age of fifteen—and the current drinking age as well. She was even too young to be gainfully employed full time. Thus, Ms. Holtz was seriously hampered in her endeavor to make her own way in the world.

Fortunately for Jo, the Nyes had graciously agreed to put her up. Taylor was only too happy to finally have a sibling in the house. They even shared the same bedroom, and now, every night was like having a sleepover. Under these circumstances, Ms. Holtz could hardly have been described as being fully autonomous, but she had been loosed from being under her parents' restrictive control, which had been her intention all along—a plan first suggested to her by Principal Nye.

Josephine was glad to be free of her parents' rules and regulations, but she never intended to cause her father to lose his job—or her mother to lose her freedom. This is why she had pled with Judge Simon for probation for her parents—although her mother's speech to the court had not so affected Josephine as to induce her to admit to having committed perjury. And she was not at all worried about having sinned against God since she longer believed in God.

But no matter how much she had seared her conscience, Josephine couldn't help feeling remorseful about how she had betrayed her parents. After all, they had only been doing what they thought was right, however misguided they were. Josephine didn't hate her parents; she only wanted to be free of them. As much as she tried not to think about it, Josephine couldn't help feeling guilty, even if Principal Nye contended that the feeling of guilt was only a conditioned biological response, based on her Christian upbringing.

Guilty feelings aside, Josephine was getting along tolerably well with her new life. She continued living with the Nye family and finished her eighth-grade year at Hillary Clinton. Jo was doing even better in school these days, thanks to her foster mother's tutelage, not to mention her nepotism, and the fact that Jo had become quite adept at regurgitating the politically correct and evolutionary-compliant verbiage on her tests.

Besides her studies, Josephine flaunted her talent as first flutist in the school concert and marching bands. This activity hardly made her the most popular of students at Clinton—playing in the school band had previously caused her to be just slightly less of a pariah than her Christianity had. However, thanks to her newfound notoriety and her secured place as Taylor Nye's best friend, Jo's popularity was decidedly on the upswing. But there was one more new development that soon put her in the upper echelon.

"Let's start a hip-bop band," Taylor suggested to Josephine one evening as the two girls were in Taylor's bedroom, listening to the local top-twenty radio station.

Hip-bop was the newest audio sensation, an odd amalgamation of the musical genres of hip-hop and bebop that was all the rage with the teen set—only old people and losers played or listened to classic rock anymore. Taylor's current beau, a very tall, lanky, fifteen-year-old, Negro/black/African American/person of color, etc., etc., lad by the name of Damien King, not only played the drums, but he could lay down a back beat that was both funky and had that swing *and* rap at the same time, which was no mean feat.

Taylor played serviceable digital piano and could supply the necessary rhythmic bedrock, allowing Josephine's soaring flute to provide the melodic voice and to be the featured soloist in the band—and she could sing well enough to augment the sound with backing vocals, when called upon. Josephine willingly agreed to the scheme, and as soon as Damien had moved his five-piece red-sparkle drum kit into the Nye's garage, the newest razz (a merging of rap and jazz) trio began to rehearse in earnest.

By mid-May, the band had moved out of the garage and was playing in the local clubs. Damien was technically an adult, and both he and Taylor (who was now fourteen) possessed driver's licenses and access to their respective parents' cars, so transportation was not a problem. And many a club or bar owner turned a blind eye to the two underage girl members when it came to their imbibing alcoholic beverages, even Josephine, who could provide legal documentation that confirmed her emancipated teen status, if need be.

Following their first gig, the trio was traveling home from the show in Damien's silver van. The young couple occupied the two front seats; Jo was sitting in the back with the equipment when she caught a whiff of a sickly-sweet smell emanating from the front compartment. After much puffing and giggling from the front seat, Taylor turned toward the rear of the vehicle and extended a small, oddly shaped cigarette, which she held by means of a metal clip.

"C'mon, Holy Holtz, have a hit," Taylor said as she offered her friend the scraggly homemade joint.

"No, thanks. I don't smoke," she said. *Holy Holtz* was the name Taylor had given to her still fairly straight bandmate.

"Aw, don't be a buzz-kill, Jo. You don't wanna be an L7, do ya?"

"An L7?" a confused Jo asked. She thought that L7 was the name an all-female alternative rock band of yesteryear.

"You know—a square," Taylor explained as she took another hit.

Jo really didn't want to toke on the proffered doobie; she didn't smoke cigarettes, nor did she often drink alcoholic beverages, but she didn't want to be labeled a square either, so she took a small puff off the strange-looking ciggy (though, much like Bill Clinton before her, she did not inhale). But even this tiny amount made her cough uncontrollably, and she handed the offending roach clip back to Ms. Nye.

Taylor took yet another hit, handed it to her boyfriend, and then laughed. "We'll make a woman out of you yet, Holy Holtz."

The band, christened Moon Goddess—the translation of Jo's first name, Cynthia (*Cyn*, meaning moon, and *thia*, meaning goddess)—was soon the talk of the town. In fact, Moon Goddess was making so many waves in the City of Water (Minneapolis, which is a combination of a Native American word for water, and *polis*, the Greek word for city) that they soon began to attract the record company sharks. The record label that they ultimately signed with was North Star Records, an homage to the state nickname, the North Star State.

Chapter 36

A Brand-New Saint

Meanwhile, back in Prairie Prison, Allie's estrangement from her cellmate proved to be only a temporary situation. Misery loves company, as the saying goes, and it was very miserable in prison. So the cellmates went back to praying together and, thanks to their finally being eligible to have their time with the prison Bible, they began to read the scriptures together as well.

One day, after Allie had prayed one of her usual prayers, which made it sound as if she knew the Creator of the universe personally, Maria said, "I simply must have the kind of relationship with God that you do."

Allie was reminded of the night when she'd led her best friend, Cindy, to the Lord. Mrs. Holtz considered the legal ramifications of breaking the proselytizing law in prison— would she be denied parole? Would she be given an even longer sentence? But she ultimately knew that she could not forsake a soul in need of salvation, so she answered.

"Well, you have to admit that you're a sinner and that Jesus Christ died on the cross for your sins."

"Ave Maria! Of course I believe that Jesus Christ died for

the sins of the world. I've recited the Apostles' Creed every Sunday for years!"

"But have you ever personalized it? Have you ever trusted in Jesus Christ's substitutionary death on the cross as the sole way to salvation?" Allie asked.

"No. I try to keep the sacraments too, of course," Maria answered.

"Faith in Jesus Christ's death on the cross for the payment of our sins is the only way to heaven," Allie preached.

"No wonder my parents warned me about people like you," Maria joked.

"The Bible says that we are saved by grace, through faith, not of works," Allie relayed.

"Where are you getting *that* from?" Maria demanded. Like a great many Roman Catholics, she knew the liturgy of the mass a lot better than she knew the Bible.

"The epistle of Paul the apostle to the Ephesians, chapter two, verses eight and nine," Allie supplied, and then she grabbed the Holy Bible off her bunk, found the pertinent passage, and handed it to her captive audience so that Maria could read it for herself.

Maria read out loud: "For by grace are ye saved through faith; and that not of yourselves: it is the gift of God: Not of works, lest any man should boast." Maria then silently read the passage over and over again, before she asked, "What does all of this mean? And what is grace?"

"Grace is God's unmerited favor; it's what you Catholics usually call mercy."

"Oh," Maria replied. "I recognize the word mercy, but to me, the word grace is either a girl's name or something that you say before meals."

"And to answer your first question, the scripture passage

means that salvation is a free gift from God. It cannot be earned—not by works, not by obeying the Old Testament law, not by 'the blood of bulls and of goats,' not by keeping the sacraments, not by performing a certain number of miracles, but only by faith in Jesus Christ alone," Allie stressed.

"I believe in Jesus Christ," Maria contended.

"Yes, but there is a big difference between believing in the fact of something and putting your faith in someone. The epistle—that means letter—of James, although you would probably call him Saint James, states that 'devils also believe, and tremble.' The difference between simple belief and saving faith is like … do you see this bunk?"

"Yes, I'm not blind, you know," Maria answered irritably.

"Well, you can say that this bunk will support your weight, but until you actually lie down on the bunk, you're not exercising true faith in it. Putting your faith in Jesus Christ means that you trust in Him alone to pay the penalty for your sins. Not in the pope, not in the sacraments, not in the Roman Catholic Church—or in any church, for that matter. You have to accept Jesus Christ as your personal Lord and Savior."

"How do I put my faith in Christ?" Maria finally asked.

"Simply pray something like this: heavenly Father, I admit that I'm a sinner, and I know that only Christ's death upon the cross can cleanse me from my sins. I accept Jesus Christ as my personal Lord and Savior. In Jesus's precious name, I pray. Amen."

Maria prayed the prayer, and immediately afterward, she felt a peace that she had never before known. Maria was so wearied from her day and so filled with the much-needed peace of the Holy Spirit now indwelling her that she simply lay down upon the very bunk that Allie had just used as a theological illustration and murmured, "Thank you, Allie. Good night."

And then she quickly succumbed to a peaceful sleep.

"Good morning, Maria," Allie said to the new convert when she awoke from her night's rest. "How did you sleep?"

"I slept like a baby," Maria answered pleasantly.

"How does it feel to be a saint?" Allie asked her.

"I'm far from being a saint," Maria protested.

"You're not as far as you may think. The word *saint* simply refers to someone who has been purified by God, one set apart for a specific purpose. According to the Bible, a saint is anyone who has accepted Jesus Christ as their Savior, *not* someone who has performed a miracle or anything like that," Allie explained.

"Really?" Maria pondered this startling new information.

"Here, look at this," Allie said as she opened up the King James Bible provided by the prison and plopped it down on "Saint" Maria's lap. "What does *this* say?"

"Paul, an apostle of Jesus Christ by the will of God, to the saints which are at Ep … Ep …" Maria stumbled.

"Ephesus," Allie supplied, and then she paged through the Bible a little further and instructed, "Now read this."

Again, Maria did as she was instructed. "Paul and Tim …"

"It's *Timotheus*," Allie pronounced. "It's Greek for Timothy. Yeah, I know; when I first started reading the New Testament it was all Greek to me too! But look at what it says a little bit below that."

"To all the saints in Christ Jesus which are at Phil …"

"Philippi." Allie once again pronounced the word for her new sister in the Lord.

"Greek for Philip?" Maria guessed.

"Close. Philippi was a city in Greece, as Ephesus was a city in Asia Minor, or what is now known as Turkey, but Philip *is* a Greek name. Now read this one, found in the book of Colossians, right after the number two."

"To the saints and faithful brethren—let me guess; more Greek?" Maria asked.

"Nope, *brethren* is King James English for brothers."

"Okay, so what's your point?" Maria wondered.

"My point is that all three of these letters, or epistles, to use the King James language, were written by the apostle Paul to different churches located in Greece and Asia Minor. Notice that he refers to the members of each of these churches as saints. Do you think he was only writing to a few people who had performed a certain number of miracles or whatever it is that you Roman Catholics claim is required for sainthood?" Allie argued.

"No, I suppose not," Maria admitted.

"It's the Holy Spirit who makes someone a saint, whenever anyone puts their faith in Jesus Christ for salvation, *not* some pope or the Roman Catholic Church."

"Oh." Maria pondered further; she was certainly getting a crash course in Protestant biblical theology that morning.

"So you really *are* a saint, Saint Maria," Allie concluded.

"Saint Maria—imagine that!" Maria contemplated joyfully.

Over the following weeks and months, Allie was overjoyed to see the change and resulting evangelistic fervor in her new sister in Christ. It made the drudgery of their sentences much more endurable. Just observing Maria's new walk by faith made Allie feel like she herself had become born again—all over again.

Chapter 37

Euphoria

Moon Goddess's debut single, "Hoppin' and Boppin'," sold like proverbial hotcakes, thanks to their record company greasing just the right palms of the radio programmers. (Whoever said that payola was dead?) A summer tour was booked, and the group was soon on their way to fame and fortune and everything that came with it—rabid fans and fan mail and publicity. But their newfound notoriety also brought with it some negative side effects—negative criticism, loss of privacy, and a loss of innocence.

As always, narcotics accompanied the music scene, and the drug dealers adhered themselves to the musicians like vultures on carrion. At first, the three members only dabbled in drugs—social drinking and pot smoking, both of which Josephine soon grew accustomed to. By then, most traditionally illegal substances had been legalized in order to tax them. The government did not want to stifle a person's recreational activities; it was far too busy restricting people's religious rights instead.

The newest wonder drug on the scene was named Euphoria. Euphoria was a synthetic drug with effects that were similar to heroin—a euphoric feeling of floating aimlessly—without the negative side effects (vomiting). It even came in a convenient pill form; no needles required. But in one aspect, Euphoria was very much like heroin: it was extremely addictive. At first, the members of Moon Goddess merely experimented with the narcotic. Damien tried it first, and then Taylor, and finally Josephine succumbed.

The first negative side effect of the drug was a musical one; the depressant had the tendency to cause tempos to drag pronouncedly. The second was social. Ironically, even though Josephine had originally succumbed due to peer pressure and a sense of band camaraderie, Euphoria was decidedly not a social drug. The more that the three of them indulged in Euphoria, the more isolated from each other they became.

Matters were not helped any by the flagging career of Moon Goddess. The music industry had long ago dispensed with releasing albums or even compact discs. Music was now made exclusively for computers, cell phones, and iPods. Nobody actually owned a physical copy of any artist's work; rather, all music was streamed onto people's devices.

In fact, there was no longer such a thing as a collection of songs released by a particular artist; only singles (most of which sounded exactly the same) were available.

Radio was still around, controlled more than ever by the strict playlists of the radio programmers (not the disc jockeys and certainly not the listeners, who were so brainwashed by the media as to be virtually devoid of an original thought), who were in service to the advertisers. But it was no longer top-forty radio; the top had been reduced to only twenty, and the top-twenty radio stations (and all radio stations were top-twenty now) just played the same twenty songs over and over again, ad nauseam.

Like any other business, the music biz was predicated on

the policy of planned obsolescence and the teenager's insatiable need to be "in." As a result, music trends changed in a matter of months, if not weeks. An artist could have the number-one record one week and the next week be yesterday's news. Hip-bop was soon replaced by hip-wop (a combination of hip-hop and do-wop). This meant that groups with guitars were out; in fact, groups that used any instruments of any kind were out.

A few months later, hip-wop would be succeeded by techno-hop, music made strictly by computers. Now groups with human beings were out. Computer programmers had become radio programmers. Live music was still around, sort of. Lip-synching was what passed for most musical entertainment. Hip-bop bands tended to play live, but once the genre was considered passé, few people cared to go see them play. In no time, Moon Goddess had gone from playing stadiums to playing small clubs.

By this time, however, Jo had ceased to care about her musical career. Although she was the last member to try Euphoria, she was the first one to really get hooked. Perhaps it was because she was the youngest or perhaps because she most needed the narcotic succor it provided. Whenever she began to experience guilty feelings over the abominable way in which she had treated her parents, one hit of Euphoria made her forget that she even had parents, much less what she'd done to them.

Soon, mundane matters, such as practicing her scales or even showing up for gigs (on time or not at all), took a back seat to getting high (or in the case of Euphoria, paralytic, if not virtually catatonic). And even when Jo deigned to show up for a show, her timing and facility on her instrument left much to be desired. The other two members carried on (and carried the gigs) as best they could, until in late August, Taylor finally confronted the floundering flutist backstage, following Moon Goddess's latest disastrous gig.

"Now the last thing I want to do is to tell anyone how to live their life," Taylor began.

"Why do I suspect there's a *but* coming?" Josephine interrupted.

"But," Taylor confirmed, "you really need to get your act together, Jo. Moon Goddess was formed as a trio, not a duo, which is essentially what we have become. Not to mention the fact that you're the band member that the group was named after. Perhaps you need a little counseling for your addiction."

"You're using too!" Josephine charged.

"I know that I sound like a hypocrite," Taylor admitted, "but there is a difference between flirting with a drug and marrying it! Damien and I need help too, but—"

"Maybe you two need help, but I don't!" Jo insisted. "So get off my back already! If I wanted to be told how to live my life, I could've stayed with my parents!"

Sensing that arguing any further would be pointless, Taylor dropped the subject.

Following Moon Goddess's one and only tour, Jo split. She not only quit the band, but she quit life as well. Fearful that even her most permissive guardians, the Nyes, would cramp her style, she moved out of their house. There was little they could do about it, as Jo was emancipated. Miss Holtz holed up in a seedy motel room and indulged in her Euphoria habit, paid for with the money that she received from royalties, which wasn't much, since the deal with North Star Records was hardly equitable.

Josephine had once played music, but all she did now was do drugs. She rarely ate, she hardly slept, she couldn't be bothered with hygiene, and she only left home to score more dope.

The emancipated teen became more and more emaciated as the weeks went by. Finally, she had a moment of clarity one morning and realized that she had to quit soon, or she would surely die. Josephine knew of one person who might be able to help her.

CHAPTER 38

Dr. McAllister, I Presume

T he Hennepin County Drug Rehabilitation Clinic was located in Minneapolis, Minnesota. It was a part of the Hennepin County Medical Center, a sprawling complex that included, in addition to the hospital and rehab center, several doctors' offices, whose practitioners ranged from general and family physicians to specialists of sundry therapeutic disciplines. Dr. Ward's office was among those housed in the facility.

The HCDRC was where Dr. Cynthia McAllister had been a drug rehab therapist for the past five years. Since narcotics were by and large legal, attending a drug rehab program was usually voluntary. But the HCDRC serviced anyone and everyone who came to them for help, including a multitude of young persons who were addicted to Euphoria, which as the trendy new drug on the market, was all the rage among the teenage set, an epidemic that put the good Dr. McAllister *in* a rage.

It had not been an easy occupational row that Dr. Cynthia McAllister had been required to hoe. After all, the field of psychology is, in many ways, the antithesis of Christianity. Sigmund Freud himself considered Christianity a form of neurosis. The very term *Christian psychologist* was considered an oxymoron in these postmodern times. But Cindy McAllister (or rather Cindy Lake, as she was known at that time) hadn't always been subject to this conundrum.

When Ms. Lake had started her undergraduate days, she was a committed pagan, a staunch feminist, and a devout syncretist. That was until her best friend and future sister-in-law, Allie Holtz led her to the Lord during her senior college year, and sinful Cindy Lake's world (and her worldview) was turned upside down. This resulted in not only Allie Holtz's first conviction, but also in Cindy developing Christian convictions.

This meant that Cindy's final semester as an undergraduate was difficult, and her postgraduate and doctoral studies were more difficult still, owing to the constant ridicule that she received from her progressive professors regarding her newfound faith. But she put in the required work to earn her degree, and the college reluctantly granted her the coveted PhD for which she had worked so very hard. But once she had that degree, she wondered exactly what she was going to do with it.

Miss Lake's original idea was to get a job as a counselor at an abortion clinic. But her conversion to Christ scuttled that particular plan. She no longer possessed a desire to coerce frightened, emotionally vulnerable women to murder their unborn babies. She would have been happy to work for the other side, except that the government had closed down all crisis pregnancy centers and had outlawed the use of ultrasound machines for prenatal examinations, lest expectant mothers should suspect the truth of when life began.

Other possible uses for her degree did not interest Cindy either, like counseling confused, impressionable children that they were really homosexual or transsexual, only because they entertained some ambivalent feelings about the opposite sex, or that they should undergo gender reassignment surgery simply because they had ambiguous feelings regarding their own gender. Worst of all, she didn't relish the prospect of trying to convince her fellow Christian believers that their faith had rendered them mentally unstable.

Not long after she earned her PhD, something occurred in Cindy's life that made her put off making a decision on which career path she should pursue. During her postgraduate years, Cindy had begun dating Allie's elder brother, Rod. It took some time after Rod had first asked her out for Cindy to regard Allie's annoying older brother with romantic feelings. Rod was like the brother that Cindy never had—and never wanted. But Rodney was good-looking, and Christian men were in short supply.

Rod and Cindy were married in the summer between the time that she earned her master's degree and before she began working on her doctorate degree; Rod had already completed his law degree. Jack Holtz served as best man, and his wife was matron of honor. Though Cindy was three months Allie's elder and had been a grade above her in school, owing to Allie's birthday falling after the school cut-off date, she was married roughly three years after Allie. Both friends had married Christian men who were older than they.

After Cindy earned her doctorate degree, she learned from Dr. Ward that she was pregnant. So she put her career on hold in order to care for her expected child—a shocking development for a former feminist like her. And she kept her career on hold until daughter Rose turned five years old and started kindergarten. Cindy's own mother wasn't about to help her in this "most disastrous" of decisions—to bear and raise a child, a decision that threatened to ruin both her figure and her career.

By the time that Rose was in school, Cindy had come to the conclusion that the only field of psychological endeavor in which she could find any redeeming qualities was drug rehabilitation. Thus, she finally began to use her PhD in this field. This way, she actually felt like she was doing some good, even though her hands were tied by the anti-proselytizing law, as far as telling her patients that the higher power they should rely on to avoid relapsing happened to be named Jesus Christ.

However, Dr. McAllister was legally allowed to refer her former patients to a qualified church (though only if the person requested it) to seek assistance from their higher power. The liberal pastors of the only government-sanctioned churches were certainly not going to preach the same gospel that they themselves did not believe in. But Cindy made it a habit to refer her former patients to the very church where Jack Holtz worked as a security guard, and *he* had no problem "making plain the way of salvation."

One day in late September, one of receptionists at the clinic informed Dr. McAllister that she'd received a phone call. Cindy told the receptionist to transfer the call to her office, and once Dr. Cindy picked up the receiver, she heard a frail, youthful voice speak tentatively.

"A-Aunt Cindy?"

"Aunt Cindy" only had one niece, so she didn't have to hazard much of a guess as to who was calling. "What do *you* want?" Cindy asked brusquely. She wasn't feeling at all charitable toward the person who'd ruined Allie's life, not to mention the mean girl who had once cruelly bullied her precious daughter, Rose.

"I … I need some help," Josephine weakly whispered.

"What sort of help?" Cindy asked suspiciously. She wasn't sure if she was on the receiving end of a "touch" from her so-called emancipated-teen relative.

"You know, the kind of help that *you* provide. I … I'm hooked on Euphoria, and I just can't stop doing it!"

Cindy could hear the catch in her young niece's voice. This softened Cindy's heart somewhat. Dr. McAllister had a ward full of Euphoria addicts, and at age fourteen, Josephine wasn't even the youngest reported case. Cindy didn't need to have anyone tell her how addictive the insidious drug was. Taking Josephine at her word, she more kindly answered,

"Well, the fact that you're willing to admit that you have a problem proves that you're not too far gone. I'll see if I can fit you in."

"Thank you," Josephine murmured.

Then the line went dead. Dr. Cynthia had to trace the call before she could even determine where to send the ambulance. Cindy managed to pull some professional strings and fit her niece into the program and into the Euphoria ward, which was already bursting at the seams with other drug casualties. But when Josephine arrived at the clinic via ambulance, Dr. McAllister reconsidered her previous statement that her niece was not "too far gone."

When she first saw her, Dr. Cindy McAllister literally gasped out loud at the alteration in her young relative. She was emaciated to the point that her bones were nearly visible through her sallow skin. She had a hollow look in her feral eyes. Her hair was falling out by the handful. And her teeth no doubt were about to follow suit (if her unattended braces hadn't still been holding them in place). Dr. Cindy didn't know if her dissipated niece would even make it through the night.

Chapter 39

When the Parole Is Called Up Yonder

Allie continued with her prison life until one day she learned that she was eligible for parole. Allie had been incarcerated for three months by then, and she had been a model prisoner (her proselytizing notwithstanding). Allie went before the three-person parole board in early July and was asked why she should be considered for parole. Allie knew that if she told the parole board what they wanted to hear, there was a good chance that they would grant her parole. But instead, she answered honestly.

"If you are asking me if I feel remorse for what I've done, as far as slapping my daughter is concerned, I regretted the action the split second after I did it. If you are asking me if I feel sorry for attempting to teach my daughter to love, respect, and obey her parents, and to love, fear, and obey God, and to respect all authority that does not force Christians to deny their faith, then my answer has to be no. I don't regret that.

"I have attempted to obey the laws of the state of Minnesota in all ways in which they do not contradict God's law. What you people must understand is that Christians like me have a higher law that we are obligated to obey. And we have religious rights that have been guaranteed by the United States

Constitution—and more important, that have been granted to us by God—that allow us to obey that higher law. Thank you."

Obviously, Allison Jane Holtz was not granted parole, and she had to serve out the rest of her sentence. No time off for good behavior for religious dissenters such as her. So Allie bided her time until early October, when her six-month prison sentence was completed. She still had her five years of probation ahead of her, but at least she could do that portion of her time on the outside.

When Allie's release finally came on October 1, she bid adieu to the other fine ladies incarcerated in Prairie Prison, including wishing her cellmate a fond farewell. Maria's "crime" had netted her a much longer sentence. Obviously, the state considered assisting expectant mothers in not murdering their unborn children was a worse offense than a mother allegedly abusing her own child.

"Goodbye, Maria. Never forget what God has done for you. And always remember that you are a saint—and that you should act accordingly."

"I will, and thank you, Allie, for explaining the gospel to me."

Allie knew that she would miss Maria, as well as the other friends that she had made on the inside. But she wasn't going to miss being in stir, nor would she miss that unflattering orange jumpsuit that she had to wear. She much preferred the street clothes that she was able to slip back into.

Allie was picked up by her husband, and after he drove her to their house, they were able to get reacquainted in the privacy of their own home. Once she settled back in, Allie wondered what she should do with her life now.

All that Allison Holtz had ever wanted to do was to be a stay-at-home mother and to raise her child in the "nurture and the admonition of the Lord." But the state had made such an endeavor impossible, and now they had robbed her of her only child. She was also forbidden to have any more children because of her conviction as a child abuser. Allie could defy the government and bear another child, but she would surely be found out eventually.

So unless Allie attempted to evade the authorities (perhaps through the aid of the underground railroad), all that her getting pregnant would accomplish was her undergoing a forced abortion or having the baby taken away and raised by the state. She could always go back to college—she had quit college once she became pregnant—and work on gaining a degree that might lead to a fulfilling career. But higher education now seemed like so much water under the bridge.

Instead, Allison got a job. It was not easy for an ex-con like her to find gainful employment, but Rod McAllister's secretary was taking maternity leave to have her one government-allotted child, and then she'd take an additional leave of absence to raise the her baby, so Rod hired his little sister to replace her. Allie could type reasonably well and rapidly so, and she was fairly organized, so she got the position, somewhat based on her abilities and not solely as a result of her brother's nepotism.

Considering her mental capabilities and her academic prowess, Allie Holtz should have expected to obtain something better than an administrative assistant's job, but she had long ago resolved to forsake college for motherhood, and she had never regretted that decision. Even if she had known in advance what trouble her daughter would go on to cause her and that she would someday lose her, if she could do it all over again, Allie would have ultimately made the same choice.

Adding insult to the Holtzes' multiplied injuries were the counseling sessions they were both required to attend as a condition of their probation. These sessions consisted of the state-approved psychologist alternately berating them for circumventing their daughter's personal autonomy and for crushing her fragile psyche with their puritanical rules and regulations, and then cajoling them to forsake their outmoded beliefs in favor of modern scientific truths.

Of course, neither Jack nor Allie would recant their faith, so the psychologist would have to conclude (in their official record) that his subjects were still not cured, and the efforts for the Holtzes' rehabilitation would continue. After each session was over, the Holtzes would return home, with Jack fuming and Allie on the verge of tears. Once inside their now emptier house, Jack would cradle his emotionally distraught wife in his arms and try to comfort her as she cried on his shoulder.

"I guess you were correct when you warned me there might be worse times ahead of us," Jack grimly said one day as he lovingly held his wife.

"I sure do wish I'd been wrong about that," Allie moaned, "but I never thought that things could get this bad. I do believe that the state was just waiting for an opportunity like this in order to take our precious child away from us, so that they could indoctrinate her with their insidious lies."

"We thought that Cindy Jo was a gift from God. 'God's special delivery,' you used to call her," Jack reminisced. "She turned out to be more like Satan's time bomb!"

"She's still God's gift to us, no matter what she has done to us," Allie countered. "God hasn't given up on her yet—and neither should we."

Chapter **40**

Give Me Twelve Steps

To Dr. McAllister's great surprise and relief, Josephine lived through the night—and for several nights thereafter. Thanks to the tender loving care of her aunt Cindy, including being administered medications designed to wean patients off Euphoria, and intravenous feeding to get her strength back up, Miss Holtz eventually began to look more human and ultimately became healthier, physically speaking. But the good doctor knew that what her patient needed most was to heal emotionally and spiritually.

The drug treatment strategy at the HCDRC was predicated on the same twelve-step program originated by Alcoholics Anonymous, which had been used in therapy for several decades. The progressive government did not object too strenuously to the use of the phrase *higher power* in the creed since the verbiage was too ambiguous to necessarily imply the God of the Bible. A higher power could be anything—a deity, the big bang, evolution, the persons themselves, or even the government itself.

Dr. McAllister was not able to make any specific suggestions to any addict, but when her patients asked her what she herself believed in, she always told them that Jesus Christ was her higher power. Josephine did not know who her own higher power was, but right now she was willing to believe in anything to kick her Euphoria habit. But it didn't take a degree in psychology for Cindy to figure out that the main reason for her niece's drug habit was her guilt.

When Josephine got to the eighth step in the process—the step where she had to make a list of all of the people she had hurt—her parents were certainly on the top of her list. When Josephine learned that step number nine was making amends to the people she had hurt, she asked her aunt/doctor, "How can I ever make amends for what I've done to my parents?"

"Well, the first thing you should do is to apologize to them. But if you really want to make amends, I would suggest that you recant your testimony against them."

"Would I get in trouble for lying under oath?" Josephine asked, worried.

"You might. You did commit perjury. You will have to decide whether or not to take that risk. But as your therapist, not to mention your aunt, I would counsel you to do the right thing."

Josephine thought about it for a number of days. Even though she had no indwelling Holy Spirit to prompt her, she still possessed a conscience. She genuinely felt remorse for what she had done to her parents. And she knew that she wanted to be truly free of her addiction and to be safeguarded against experiencing a relapse. So she told her aunt and therapist, during their next meeting together, "Okay, I'll do it. I'll do the right thing. I'll recant my testimony."

"Good for you, Cindy Jo." Cindy encouraged her namesake with a hug. "I'm proud of you—for the first time in a very long time."

But doing the right thing was not so simple. Josephine couldn't even meet with her parents face-to-face before she'd stated in writing that she was initiating contact with them. So Rodney J. McAllister, attorney-at-law (and uncle), obtained a signed deposition from his newly repentant niece, not only granting her parents permission to have an audience with their own daughter but also recanting her false testimony against them.

Rod and Cindy McAllister were hoping that this new testimony would force Judge Simon to reverse his decision and to commute the Holtzes' sentences—or at least to grant Lawyer McAllister's request for a new trial. However, when Rod presented Judge Simon with the affidavit, the judge did none of these things. Instead, he simply requested a meeting with young Ms. Cynthia Josephine Holtz. Josephine and her uncle and aunt met with the Honorable Daniel Simon in his chambers, where he adjured her.

"Ms. Cynthia Josephine Holtz, do you swear that this revised testimony is the truth, the whole truth, and nothing but the truth?"

"Yes, Your Honor," Josephine answered.

Judge Simon wrinkled his brow, drummed his fingers on his desk, and contemplated this new development for a short while. Then he said, "Hmm ... even if I did not highly suspect that the young, impressionable Ms. Holtz may have been unduly influenced by her elder relatives and that this reversal of her testimony has been coerced, there is still the testimony of Principal Nye and her daughter to consider. Thus, I am not inclined to grant a mistrial or a new trial on these grounds. However, if Ms. Holtz wishes to meet with her parents, she has every right, as an emancipated teen, to do so. The Holtzes are granted permission to see their daughter."

As the three dejected souls left the courthouse together, Rod groused, "His Honor just didn't want to admit that the judicial system had made an error. But at least he granted our petition for a meeting, so we have won a small victory."

The meeting was arranged for mid-November in the lobby of the HCDRC (and in the presence of the Holtzes' parole officer). The Holtzes found Josephine even gaunter than usual, and her hair was cut a little shorter than before, but she was still their daughter. The resulting conversation was understandably stilted.

"How are you feeling?" Allie asked her daughter.

"Fine, all things considered," Josephine answered.

"That's good," Allie responded and then thought, *That was lame.*

A pregnant pause ensued, broken only by Josephine's heartfelt admission.

"I'm so sorry for what I did to you."

"We forgave you for that a long time ago," Jack Holtz said.

Josephine could tell by the looks on her parents' faces that this was true, and she marveled at it. She had heard all about forgiveness while growing up, but actually experiencing such forgiveness in practice was quite different than in theory. Jo ran over to her mother and hugged her tightly. It was the first loving act that she had bestowed on her mother in many months.

"Thank you, Mommy," Josephine murmured. Then she hugged her daddy as well.

After the meeting was over, Jack and Allie took their leave. Jack observed to his overjoyed wife, "That went well. And that apology seemed genuine."

"I hope for Cindy Jo's sake that it was genuine," Allie commented. "Maybe there is hope for our unsaved daughter yet."

CHAPTER 41

Genuine Repentance

Once Jo completed her rehabilitation in early December, she wondered what to do next. Her musical career was over, and she had missed the first semester of her freshman year of high school while she was mired in her drug addiction and subsequent drug rehab. *So now what?* she thought. *Go back to school? Go back to living with the Nyes?* Although if she was once again paired with the bad influence that was Taylor Nye, would she also soon be back under the harmful influence of Euphoria?

Jo may have been an emancipated teen, but she sure didn't feel like an adult. She felt more like a frightened little girl. She could conceivably do anything that she wanted to do, as long as it wasn't against the law, but ironically after all of the trouble she'd gone through—and put her parents through—to gain her freedom, all that she wanted to do now was go back home and be taken care of by those same parents. After wanting to live a life without borders, she now longed for a stable environment.

But even if her parents had forgiven her from their hearts, would they go so far as to welcome her back with open arms? Josephine asked her aunt Cindy to approach her parents to broach the subject. To her great surprise and joy, her parents agreed to the arrangement. Once again, Josephine had to legally put her desires into writing. But once she had, she moved back into her old house; she even moved back into her old bedroom.

Her bedroom had been kept in pristine condition in her absence. Resting upon her bed was the Holy Bible that her parents had bought for her twelfth birthday; this was also in pristine condition, owing to the fact that she had hardly cracked the book's cover since she'd first received it (having already apostated in her heart by then). Curious, Josephine picked the book up, opened the cover, and read the inscription inside.

To our precious daughter, Cindy Jo,
God's special delivery to us.
May you always remain true to your Christian faith.
Love,
Mom and Dad

Cindy Jo burst into tears. She held the Bible tightly to her chest as she wept profusely. *I certainly haven't remained true to my Christian faith, have I?*

As Josephine settled back into her old life, adjustments had to be made. There was now a palpable tension and unease residing in the Holtz house. Mr. and Mrs. Holtz walked on eggshells whenever Josephine was around them, wary that they might once again incur the wrath of their truculent daughter, which would then cause her to go to Principal Nye to rat out her parents to the progressive powers that be.

For her part, Josephine was at a loss as to what to say to her parents. *Sorry* seemed such a trite and insufficient word after the abominable way she had treated them. So the elephant stayed permanently parked in whatever room they happened to be in. Josephine went out of her way to be the dutiful daughter that she hadn't always been, and her parents treated her with polite kindness and gentleness in return, their love and forgiveness showing through in their every action toward her.

Josephine's emotions were a jumble—comfort and joy at being back home but intense guilt over what she had done to her parents. At first, her parents' kindness made her feel even guiltier, so much so that Josephine was sorely tempted to score some more euphoria just to have its calming effects temporarily take away her feelings of remorse. But in time, she began to see her parents' forgiveness in light of what she had been taught as a child regarding God's eternal love and unmerited favor.

She also began to understand that everything that her parents had done to her (or rather, for her) had been done out of love. She used to chafe under her parents' restrictive restraints, not realizing that they had been put in place to protect her. Jo's freedom had wrought nothing but destruction in her life, which could have been avoided if she'd kept to the narrow way. Josephine began to contemplate that the Holy Bible was not just a collection of fairy tales, but rather, it was the truth—much truer than the Nyes' lies.

Obviously, Josephine had heard the gospel several times while growing up; she had even prayed the sinner's prayer when she was a child, due to a combination of her fear of hell and to tell her parents what they'd wanted to hear. But it was also obvious that she had never believed the gospel. But now that she was older and had a real need for forgiveness, she felt the conviction of the Holy Spirit and the necessity of repentance. In the privacy of her bedroom, Josephine knelt down in front of her bed and prayed.

"Father, I don't know if You can even forgive me for all of

the horrible things that I've done—blaspheming Your name, dishonoring my parents, bearing false witness, and any other of Your commandments that I may have broken. But please do forgive me of my sins! And may my conversion be genuine this time. I ask this in the glorious name of Your precious Son, Jesus Christ. Amen."

Josephine's conversion was genuine this time; she could tell by the overwhelming sense of peace and joy she'd experienced immediately following that prayer. After her spiritual regeneration, she wanted to run into the living room and announce to her parents, "I'm saved!" But she knew that they'd heard that all before. She had once claimed to have accepted Jesus Christ as her personal Lord and Savior, but it was patently obvious that she had never truly been born again.

So why should her parents believe her now? How would they know that it really took this time, unless their daughter displayed "fruits in keeping with repentance"? Jo decided to let her actions speak louder than her words, much like her aunt Cindy had done years before, by her new obedient and joyful attitude toward them.

One morning, days later, Josephine came into the kitchen while her mother was fixing breakfast.

"Good morning, Cin—er, Josephine," her mother greeted her.

"Cindy is fine," she said pleasantly. "I prefer Josephine, but I'm not going to make a federal case over it—not like I did last time."

"You know, Josephine, considering the way that you've

been acting lately, if I didn't know better, I'd suspect that my daughter has truly become a Christian."

"I *have* truly become a Christian." Cindy/Josephine beamed. "This time for real! And I'm so sorry for what I did to you and Daddy."

"We've already forgiven you for that and so has the Lord. It's about time that you forgive yourself as well," Allie advised her genuinely repentant daughter.

Chapter 42

Rehabitual Liar

Following much contemplation, Josephine decided to keep going by her middle name. She really preferred the name, even if she had once used the moniker as a sign of her rebellion. But she figured that not every Saul had to be renamed as Paul; after all, Apollos, a name no doubt derived from the Greek god Apollo, had kept his original name. Besides, she figured that if Jesus Christ could redeem her soul, then He could also redeem her name as well.

After celebrating a pleasant Christmas (or Winter Solstice Season) with her parents (her first Christmas as a true believer), it was time for Josephine to return to school. She had missed an entire semester and she had much homework to make up in order to catch up with her fellow students at Barack Obama High School. But when she started school in January, she was surprised to discover the absence of her former best friend forever, Taylor Nye. She soon discovered the reason why.

Aunt Cindy called her up one day in January and told her that she had a new patient in the Euphoria wing at the rehab clinic—named Taylor Nye. Dr. McAllister suggested that Miss Holtz might prove to be a positive role model for Miss Nye (and a listening ear). Josephine agreed to the scheme, and one

Saturday afternoon she drove down to the Hennepin County Medical Center with her newly acquired driver's license and a car borrowed from her mother.

While she was walking into the rehab clinic, Ms. and Mrs. Nye were walking out. Josephine hadn't seen Taylor's parents since she'd moved out; she had been wary of coming under their influence again.

A surprised Principal Nye greeted her.

"Oh! Hi, Josephine. How are you doing these days?"

"Fine," Josephine answered warily.

"I hear that you are back at home, living with your parents," Bobbie said.

"Yes," Josephine confirmed, unsure of exactly how to take the question.

"Well, I guess that your parents' trial was a waste of the taxpayers' money!" Bobbie Nye laughed.

Josephine nervously twirled a lock of her flaming red hair while she fidgeted. What was Principal Nye implying? That she would have been better off if she had stayed with the Nyes? Josephine certainly didn't think so! But Bobbie was right about one thing: the trial had been a waste of the taxpayers' money since her parents had never abused her (other than according to the ridiculous anti-spanking law).

Perhaps sensing Josephine's discomfort, Joyce Foster-Nye pleasantly inquired, "So you've gone through this treatment yourself?"

"Yes, I have," Josephine confirmed, relieved to have moved on to a new topic.

"Then the program worked in your case?" Joyce asked.

"Yes, it did."

"Then hopefully it will work for Taylor too," Joyce said.

"It should," Joyce's wife interposed. "After all, according

to your aunt, Dr. Cynthia McAllister, Taylor was nowhere near as far gone as you were. We mostly brought her here as a preemptive strike before she got too addicted to Euphoria."

"That was wise," Jo said, "though ultimately it was my conversion to Jesus Christ that really made the difference."

Bobbie sighed. "I was afraid this would happen if you moved back home. I suppose that you're once again under your religious-nut parents' collective thumbs."

"Better than being under the harmful sway of Euphoria addiction," Jo shot back.

Thankfully, Joyce Foster-Nye's cooler head prevailed, and she halted the argument which was quickly brewing. "You'll have to forgive my wife's outburst, Josephine. I think that she's only worried about our daughter's welfare." She shot a pointed look at her wife.

Bobbie pasted on a fake smile and said with exaggerated politeness, "Yes, this is obviously neither the time nor the place for this discussion. Thank you for coming to visit our daughter, Josephine."

"Hopefully, it will do her a world of good," Joyce added.

"Goodbye, Nyes. I will pray for your family," Josephine promised.

"Don't waste your time on that nonsense on our account," Bobbie retorted.

"Thank you for your prayers," Joyce said, much more good-naturedly, "but we really must be going. Come along, Bobbie."

Bobbie resisted the urge to comment further, and instead, she obeyed her wife and departed with her.

Josephine found Taylor's hospital room, where Taylor lying in bed, looking a little worse for wear.

When Taylor saw her friend, she exclaimed, "Jo! I hoped you'd come visit me!"

"Of course I'm going to visit my best friend," Jo replied as she hugged her and then sat down in a nearby chair. "So how are you feeling?"

"I'm a little shaky, actually," Taylor answered.

"So was I when I was admitted here. In fact, I was a lot shaky."

"You were at death's door, according to your aunt," Taylor replied. "You were in a much worse state than I am, I understand."

"Yes, I was," Josephine admitted, "but I feel very confident about my chances of not relapsing."

"That gives me some hope," Taylor replied, "So what's your secret, then?"

"Well, believe it or not, it's … Jesus Christ. He is my higher power."

Taylor chortled. "So you've fallen back on that crutch, eh? You're not going to start proselytizing me like your mother did to your aunt, are you?"

"No, I'm only answering your question," Josephine said defensively.

"Don't worry, Jo. I'm not going to turn you in or anything," Taylor promised.

"Thank you. How are you doing with the twelve-step program?"

"I think it's rather silly," Taylor opined, "all of this business about a higher power. I don't need any higher power to kick my Euphoria habit."

"What about steps eight and nine?" Josephine asked.

"What about them? I have nothing to make amends for," Taylor contended.

"How about your lying under oath?" Josephine asked pointedly.

"Oh, so that's what this is all about. I thought that you came here to see me, for my own sake, not to try to get your parents off the hook!"

"I did come to see you for your own sake. But if you really want to get well, you will eventually have to admit that you've done wrong, and then you'll have to make amends for those wrongs."

"Right and wrong are simply moral concepts. They don't come into play in the real world of survival of the fittest. I feel no guilt whatsoever for what I did to achieve our aim of extricating you from your parents' puritanical clutches. Sorry if you don't feel the same way. My only disappointment is that it appears it was all for naught, since you've willingly moved back into that oppressive environment. But I think I need to rest now, so I would appreciate it if you'd just leave. Thank you so very much for coming."

Josephine was a bit miffed by Taylor's curt dismissal, but she remained gracious to the end. "Goodbye, Tay. I'll pray for you," Jo promised as she got up to leave.

"If you think it'd do any good," Taylor answered as she returned her friend's hug.

Considering Taylor's resolution to deny her guilt in the matter, particularly to herself, Josephine left the clinic unsure if her visit had done Taylor any good.

Chapter 43

Unexpectedly Expecting

As it turned out, Taylor was able to kick her drug habit without the aid of a higher power and without much adherence to the famed twelve steps, and she was back in school by February. Despite their theological differences and the fact that Josephine's newfound faith made her infinitely less popular at school than Taylor, the two girls remained friends. Taylor often teased Jo over her beliefs, but she no longer bullied her. Sometimes, however, Taylor's attitude could be downright hostile.

"Why do you hate Christians so much?" an exasperated Josephine asked her one Friday evening in mid-May during a sleepover at the Holtz house.

"Because Christians hate people like my parents!" Taylor angrily retorted.

"My parents don't hate anybody, including your parents," Josephine said. "They might not agree with their lifestyle, but—"

"That's the same thing as hating them," Taylor said, quoting the progressive party line.

"No, it isn't," Josephine argued. "I disagree with you about a whole lot of things, but that doesn't mean that I hate you. And I hope that you don't hate me either."

"No, I don't hate you. But you sure do annoy me at times!" Taylor said with obvious platonic affection.

"Christianity is not a religion of hate; it's all about love," Josephine preached, "the love of God for a world full of sinful, rebellious people—like I was."

"I don't believe in the concept of sin," Taylor said. "Anyway, I couldn't become a Christian even if I wanted to. My parents would never forgive me!"

"Wouldn't it be better to have God's forgiveness than that of your parents?"

"I suppose so, if I actually believed in God, which I don't."

"How else do you explain life on this planet?" Josephine asked.

"Mother Bobbie says that space aliens visited this planet billions and billions of years ago," Taylor patiently explained.

"Okay, then how do you explain the existence of these space aliens?"

"Good question. But even if I believed that there was a Creator, that doesn't mean that I have to believe in your Christian God."

Josephine didn't press the point as the two girls bedded down for the night, and the sleepover continued on a less contentious note.

The next morning, Taylor seemed more pensive and less argumentative than usual.

As Josephine was making up her bed, she said, "You're awfully quiet this morning, Tay. Is there anything wrong?"

Taylor took a deep breath and then said, "I went to the doctor a few weeks ago, and I found out that I'm pregnant."

Josephine gasped. "How did this happen?"

"I know that your parents are conservative Christians and all, but surely you must have learned all about this in biology class," Taylor teased.

"Of course I'm familiar with the facts of life, silly. I meant how did you specifically become pregnant?"

"Well, Damien and I—"

"That's enough! TMI, Tay!" Josephine interrupted, "So Damien's the father."

"Naturally," Taylor confirmed blithely.

"So, what are you going to do about it?"

"Get an abortion, of course," Taylor answered matter-of-factly. "What else?"

"Taylor, no!" Josephine exclaimed. "That would be murder!"

"Meat is murder; abortion is a woman's constitutional right," Taylor quoted.

"Do you honestly believe that killing an animal is worse than killing a human being?" Josephine asked.

"What's the difference, Jo? Humans are animals. We're nothing more than a highly evolved ape." Taylor once again had quoted her mother Bobbie.

"Mankind is a special creation of God. We are all made in His image, including the unborn child that you're now carrying," Josephine pointed out.

"The ol' crown of creation doctrine, eh?" Taylor sneered. "And by the way, *mankind* is a sexist term!"

"Whatever. Listen, Tay, please think about what you're going to do!" Josephine pleaded with her.

"I have thought about it. My parents and I have calmly discussed the situation extensively, and we've all agreed that (a) I'm much too young to take care of a baby; (b) it may be potentially dangerous to bear children at my age, and (c) I shouldn't waste my one government-approved chance at having a child on this accident."

"What about your child's one chance at life?" Josephine countered.

"It's too late, Jo. My parents have already scheduled the appointment."

Sensing that she was losing the battle, Josephine decided to call out the big guns. "Is it all right if I tell my mother about this?"

"Sure," answered Taylor, "alert the media. What do I care? Unplanned pregnancies are no longer the stigmas that they once were—and neither are abortions."

Josephine then grabbed her best friend by the hand, led her out of her bedroom and into the kitchen, where her mother was preparing breakfast, and sat her down on one of the kitchen chairs. After Josephine informed her mother of Taylor's bad decision, Mrs. Holtz attempted, over breakfast, to dissuade the young mother-to-be from her plan to not be a mother.

Allie figured that persuading the recently turned fifteen-year-old pagan to choose life was a futile gesture, but she at least had to try. "Taylor, I know that we don't see eye to eye about ... well, anything, but would you please reconsider your decision to abort your baby?"

"It's not a baby; it's a fetus," Taylor argued.

"*Fetus* is actually derived from a Latin word meaning baby," Mrs. Holtz informed her guest.

"Oh. Well, *whatever* it is, I've already decided to abort it."

"Before you do, could you please look at some literature?" Allie asked her.

"Sure," Taylor answered with a shrug of her adolescent shoulders.

Allie went back to the master bedroom and pulled out

the bottom drawer of her dresser. Underneath the drawer was a secret compartment where she hid government-banned material, including everything that she possessed regarding prenatal development. Allie knew that she was taking a chance; even having such data was a serious offense, let alone showing them to an unbeliever who would most probably rat her out as soon as look at her.

But Allie just couldn't stand the thought of yet another innocent life being snuffed out needlessly for the sake of convenience, not if she could do anything about it. So she took the risk of once again landing in prison (for her third strike this time), and she brought out the illegal information to show to the incorrigible miscreant who had already once before put her in legal hot water by falsely testifying against her in court.

Taylor perused the material and simply asked, "How do I know if any of this stuff you've shown me is true?"

Allie answered enigmatically, "Wait here; I'll be right back." Mrs. Holtz left the room, and when she came back, she said, "There is one more thing that I can show you later this evening, which may change your mind, if you would be willing to see it."

"Sure," Taylor repeated noncommittally.

Later, while Jack worked his night security job at the church, Allie drove the two adolescent girls over to the Hennepin County Medical Center. The three women were let into a rear door of the largely empty edifice by Dr. Ward, who asked Mrs. Holtz, "Are you sure that you want to go through with this, Allie?"

"In for a penny, in for a pound," Allie grimly answered.

Chapter 44

Abort the Abortion

Dr. Ward led the small party down a sparsely lit hallway to a freight elevator, which took them farther down to the basement. Once there, they walked down another darkened hallway until they came to a locked door. Dr. Ward unlocked the door and let them in. She turned on the light and then locked the door again.

Inside the room was an examination table, some metal folding chairs, and a strange looking machine.

Josephine pointed at the apparatus. "What is that thing?"

"That thing," Dr. Ward answered, "is something that will most likely land the adults present here in jail."

"Most probably," Allie acknowledged ruefully, "and I thank you for agreeing to take that risk with me, Dr. Ward."

"It's a far cry from over fourteen years ago, when I advised you to abort this lovely creature," Dr. Ward said, placing her hand tenderly on Josephine's head.

"You weren't a Christian back then," Allie pointed out.

"And I probably wouldn't be a Christian today if you hadn't witnessed to me."

The good physician had been changed greatly by the Great Physician.

"What's so great about being a Christian?" Taylor asked.

Just then, they were joined by a young woman dressed in a white lab coat. She had short pale-blonde hair and gray eyes, and she possessed a passing resemblance to Cindy Lake at that age.

"Daphne, I'm glad that you could make it," Dr. Ward said in greeting. "Allie, this is Daphne Cates. Miss Cates is also a believer, and she is specifically trained for this type of procedure."

"Well, we'd better get started. The longer we delay, the better chance that we have of getting caught," the registered diagnostic medical sonographer wisely advised them.

The procedure began. Miss Cates applied a gel to Taylor's abdomen and then placed a small wand, known as a transducer, there and moved it over the surface of Miss Nye's somewhat protruding belly, which produced a black-and-white image on the monitor.

When Taylor saw the ghostly figure emerge on the screen, she gasped. "What is that?"

"That is what our government so blithely refers to as inanimate tissue, a lump of flesh, a fetus," Daphne answered, "and that sound you're hearing is the baby's heartbeat."

Taylor watched the decidedly active shape with awe. Finally, she spoke up. "That's not a lump of flesh at all; it's alive!"

"It's alive, it's human, and it has been created in the image of God," Allie added.

Taylor watched the image a while longer, captivated, until she quietly said, mostly to herself, "They've *lied* to me." Finally, Taylor turned to the other women and resolutely told them, "I can't kill this baby that's growing inside of me. It would be murder!"

Josephine flung her arms around her friend. "Good for you, Tay."

"But what am I going to tell my parents?"

"*Please* don't tell them about the—whatever that thing is," Josephine said.

"It's an ultrasound," Daphne said, "also known as a sonogram."

Prenatal use of ultrasound machines had been banned by the government.

"I won't tell anyone what we did tonight," Taylor promised. "I wouldn't want any of you to get into trouble."

The three adult women breathed a collective sigh of relief.

"I guess I'll just have to think of something," Taylor said.

"Something that does not involve lying, I hope," Allie said.

Then the party stealthily exited the room. Dr. Ward locked the door again, and one freight-elevator ride later, the group departed from the medical center and left in their respective automobiles. Taylor spent the rest of Saturday night over at the Holtz house.

After lunch the next day, Taylor bade the Holtzes a fond farewell and then drove back over to her parents' house.

Allie informed her husband what she had done the previous evening.

"You were taking quite a chance on a girl who once told lies about us—and under oath at that!" Jack reminded his wife.

"I know, but I just couldn't stand idly by and watch another innocent life be taken for the sake of convenience, even if it is sanctioned and encouraged by our government."

"Ordered by the government, after the first child," Jack

said. "It's ironic that the liberals used to say that it was a woman's right to choose to have an abortion, and now the liberal government has virtually taken away the woman's right to *not* choose to have an abortion. You did the right thing, Allie. 'We ought to obey God rather than men,' particularly when these men 'make haste to shed innocent blood.'"

The Holtz family spent much of that Sunday afternoon in sweet fellowship at home. Jack and Allie could no longer attend the services at Billie McAllister's house, lest they have any contact with their underage niece, Rose, and thus violate their parole. Jo had made peace with her cousin, though, following her true conversion to Christ. Mrs. McAllister was overjoyed that her granddaughter had come back to the faith—or had finally come to faith in Christ for the first time, to be more accurate.

Sunday evening found the Holtz family still at home, engaged in their respective leisure activities—woodworking in the garage for Jack, reading the Bible for Allie, searching the web for Josephine—when their repose was interrupted by the ringing of their doorbell. Josephine opened the front door to the sight of Taylor Nye, standing on their doorstep, with a couple of suitcases, one on each side of her.

"May I please come in?" she asked. "My parents just threw me out!"

Not wanting to turn away a soul in need, the Holtzes agreed to let Taylor stay, at least for the night. The Holtz family helped move all of Taylor's worldly possessions—which she had brought over in the car that she'd bought with the proceeds from her musical career—into Josephine's room. After Taylor had settled in, Josephine asked her what had happened.

"After I got home and worked up the courage, I told my parents that I just didn't feel right about having the abortion, that what was growing inside of me was a real person, and that I was going to keep my baby. Mom Bobbie claimed that I was spending far too much time at the Holtz house, and she forbade me from having any further contact with you and your fanatical family because you were a bad influence on me. Then she sent me to my room, without any Sunday dinner, to think it over.

"Mom Joyce visited me later and said that they were only concerned about my welfare and that they didn't want me to ruin my life—she was playing good cop to Bobbie's bad cop. After several hours in my room, my parents gave me one more chance to come to my senses and to act responsibly. But I didn't change my mind. I *couldn't*, not after what I'd seen. Then Mother Bobbie gave me an ultimatum: if I was to continue to live under their roof, then I would have to obey them. So I made my choice, and I left."

The Holtz family agreed to let Taylor stay with them for the time being, given the present circumstances. With Ms. Taylor Nye having recently turned fifteen years old, it did not violate the conditions of Jack and Allie's parole, and as a qualified adult, Taylor was free to stay with anyone she chose. So Taylor stayed with the Holtz family (who had now become her host family) for the duration of her pregnancy.

Chapter 45

From Here to Maternity

While Taylor boarded with the Holtz family, Rod McAllister took down a written deposition from her in which she recanted her testimony, which he then presented before Judge Simon. The Honorable Daniel Simon once again looked suspiciously at the document, but with two recantations in the case, he was finally forced to do something. Judge Simon still refused to admit that his judgment was in error, however, so he also refused to revoke his guilty verdict.

Instead, Judge Simon commuted the Holtzes' sentences to time served and suspended their parole. Bobbie Nye hired a lawyer and attempted to legally force Taylor to submit to an abortion, but the judge of that case, the Honorable Gloria Dawson, decided that since Taylor was legally an adult, she was competent enough to make this decision for herself, and Judge Dawson ruled against the Nyes.

Despite her resolve to do the right thing, Taylor entertained weak moments during the entire five months that were left of her pregnancy, when it all seemed simpler to just give in to her parents' wishes and abort her baby. After all, she did want to finish high school and to go on to college, dreams that seemed rather remote with the prospect of being a teenage mother.

But when she voiced these thoughts to Mrs. Holtz, Allie exclaimed, "You can't have an abortion—not now, when you've come so far!"

"Fine. If you want me to have this baby so badly, then *you* can take care of it!"

"I would love to take care of your child, Taylor. But I doubt that the state would allow it, owing to my conviction as child abuser," Allie pointed out.

"Then what about Dr. McAllister?" Taylor asked, seemingly grasping at straws.

"My brother and his wife? It's possible that they would be willing."

The day of reckoning finally arrived in late October, and Taylor went to the Hennepin County Medical Center to have her baby. At her relatively young age, the procedure was far from a slam-dunk. The presiding physician was of the opinion that a simple abortion would be a much better course of action than for Taylor to go through the pains and pangs of labor, but he didn't want to impinge upon the mother-to-be's personal autonomy in the matter, so he did not press the point.

Taylor was kept in a hospital room while she waited for the time between her contractions to lessen enough to indicate that she was ready to give birth. The Holtzes and McAllisters rallied around her, including Ma McAllister. Neither one of Taylor's parents were there for moral support, as fitting punishment for her disobedience. But the expectant father was there. At one point, Taylor asked to speak to Josephine alone. The gathered throng exited the hospital room to give the friends some privacy.

"Jo, I'm really scared. What if I die during childbirth?" Taylor asked.

"You don't have to be afraid of death, Tay, not if you know where you're going."

"How can you be so sure of where you're going when you die?"

"I have faith in what the Holy Bible teaches," Josephine answered simply.

"Well, I have faith in what Charles Darwin taught," Taylor countered.

"Look at it this way: if you're right, then when you die, you'll become worm food. But if I'm right, then 'it is appointed unto men once to die, but after this the judgment.'"

"There you go using that sexist term *men* again," Taylor joked grimly, "but that's what worries me—that you're right, and I'm wrong. 'Conscience does make cowards of us all,' and I'm afraid of what I may find in that 'undiscovered country.'"

"You could find joy everlasting in heaven, if only you would trust in Jesus Christ's substitutionary death upon the cross to pay for your sins."

A pregnant pause ensued before nine-months-pregnant Taylor answered quietly, "Well, I don't want to die and go to hell, if there really is such a place. And I do feel sorry for what I did to your parents. Was that a sin?"

"Yes, it was. And Christ died for that sin and for all of your other sins too."

Taylor was again quiet and pensive for a time. Then she asked, "What do I have to do?"

"Just repent of your sins—er, tell God that you're sorry for what you've done. And that you believe that Jesus Christ, His Son, paid for all of your sins."

Taylor prayed for the first time ever. "Okay. God, I don't

know if you really exist, but if you do, then please forgive me for all of my sins."

"How do you feel now?" Josephine asked her.

"I'm no longer afraid," Taylor replied joyfully.

Taylor went into the delivery room, while her friends, most of whom were now her spiritual family, waited in the waiting room. Since Dr. Laura Ward and Daphne Cates worked in the complex, they also dropped by to offer moral support.

Suddenly, there was a great commotion, and one of the maternity nurses came out to inform the group that there had been complications during the procedure and that the patient was hemorrhaging. "Worst of all, we are all out of B-negative blood," said the nurse. "B-negative is one of the least common of all blood types."

"I'm B negative," Allie said.

"Would you be willing to submit to a blood transfusion?" the nurse asked.

"Yes, of course I would," Allie answered without hesitation or reservation.

Allie's blood was checked to determine if it matched the patient's—it did—and she was prepped for the procedure. Meanwhile, her husband organized a prayer meeting in the hospital's interfaith chapel. Even with the transfusion, there was no guarantee that they wouldn't lose the patient, or her baby, or both! They were soon joined by none other than Joyce Foster-Nye, who had defied her wife's edict and had come to the hospital anyway. When she was apprised of the situation, the agitated mother cried, "That should be me in there giving my blood, not Ms. Holtz! I also have B-negative blood, and I'm

Taylor's mother. I should have come sooner, no matter what Bobbie said."

Then Joyce broke down. Both Mrs. McAllisters put their comforting arms around her, and all of the Christians present took turns praying for her daughter and for her unborn child (and for Allie too). Thank God, the effectual fervent prayer of these righteous men and women availed much, because after several harrowing moments, one of the maternity nurses came into the chapel.

"Both the mother and the child have pulled through," she informed the gathered group. "The doctor believes that both of them and Mrs. Holtz will be all right. Oh, by the way—it's a boy!"

There ensued much joy and thankfulness to God for that good news. Once it quieted down some, a tearful Mrs. Foster-Nye commented, "I don't understand. After everything that my family has done to yours, why would Mrs. Holtz give her own blood to save my daughter's life? Is it only because she cares so much about saving the life of Taylor's unborn child?"

"Every life is precious to us, both Taylor's and her baby's life, because all life is made in the image of God," Jack explained. "But Allie giving her blood to save Taylor and her child was nothing compared to Jesus Christ shedding His precious blood to pay for the sins of the whole world."

Joyce took the statement in and then quietly replied, "It appears that Bobbie and I may have misjudged you people."

Taylor was wheeled into a room in the maternity ward, and eventually she was presented with her newborn baby, whom she christened Shane Allen Nye. Though weakened by her ordeal, Ms. Nye nevertheless proudly showed off her offspring to Damien and to Grandmother Joyce, both of whom immediately fell in love with him, and to anyone else in the medical center who cared to see him.

Allie was transferred to another room in the medical center to rest from the blood transfusion. Various family members visited her, including her husband and her daughter.

"How are you feeling?" Jack asked lovingly.

"As well as can be expected, under the present circumstances. I feel a little weak, physically speaking, though I'm feeling rather joyful, emotionally speaking!"

"As well you should. That was a very Christlike thing for you to do. I've never been prouder of you," Allie's mother said.

"I agree," Jack said. "It was even more impressive than when you went to court over sharing your faith."

"Or when I went to prison for disciplining my child?" Allie asked impishly.

Josephine hung her head in shame and mumbled, "That was entirely my fault."

Allie cupped her right hand under her daughter's chin, gently lifted Josephine's face upward, and then tenderly said, "You meant it for evil, but God meant it for good."

"What good could've possibly come from what I did to you?" Josephine asked.

"For one thing, I led my cellmate to the Lord," Allie answered, "not to mention that my experience in prison aided me in becoming more conformed to the image of Jesus Christ."

Just then, Joyce Foster-Nye tentatively entered the room and nervously said, "Mrs. Holtz, I wanted to thank you for what you did for my family and to apologize for what we did to you and your family. We really believed that what we were doing was best for Josephine at that time."

"And you no longer feel that way?" Jack asked.

"I'm not sure what to think now," Joyce answered truthfully. "I've always believed that Christians like you were horrible people, but perhaps I was wrong about that."

Allie laughed. "Well, that's an improvement, at least. I'd like to believe that I'm not too horrible of a person."

"If anyone is a horrible person around here, it's me," Josephine said.

"We've already forgiven you, Cindy Jo," Allie reminded her once again. "And we've already forgiven you too, Joyce, and Bobbie and Taylor—a long time ago."

"Thank you," Joyce mumbled uncomfortably.

"How is Taylor doing?" Cindy asked.

"Both mother and child are doing fine," a relieved Mrs. Nye answered.

"May I see them?" Josephine asked.

Joyce took Josephine's hand in hers. "Let me take you to both of them—actually to all three of them: mother, father, and child."

"Goodbye, Cindy Jo. I love you," Allie called out after her. "And I'm so proud of the fine young Christian lady that you've become."

"I love you too, Mama," Josephine replied.

After Joyce led Josephine out of the room, Allie turned to her husband. "She has really turned out to be God's special delivery to us after all."

"As arrows are in the hand of a mighty man, so are children of the youth. Happy is the man that hath his quiver full of them," Jack quoted.

"Well, thanks to our progressive government, we're only allowed to fill our quiver with one arrow," his wife wryly observed, "but thank God, this particular child turned out to be a straight arrow in the end."

Chapter 46

Epilogue
The Children of Obedience

Following the birth of her child, Taylor decided to keep baby Shane, even if it meant dropping out of school, a prospect that hardly pleased her two mothers, Bobbie especially. Damien did the right thing and made an honest woman out of Taylor, and Josephine served as the maid of honor at their wedding. Damien soon began working as a recording engineer to support his family. He eventually came to faith in Christ as well, so the couple was not "unequally yoked" for too long.

Taylor subsequently earned her GED, thanks to the babysitting services of her biological mother, Joyce. Bobbie refused outright to support her daughter's politically incorrect scheme to choose motherhood over a career. Eventually, thanks to the witness of her daughter, Joyce Foster-Nye also repented of her sins and accepted Jesus Christ as her personal Lord and Savior. Naturally, Joyce Foster's decision for Christ ultimately precipitated the dissolution of the Nyes' marriage.

As the woman scorned, Bobbie Nye unleashed her hellish fury by threatening to take the entire Holtz family to court over their alienating the affections of her wife, until Joyce and Taylor finally convinced her that if she ever truly loved them, she would honor their wishes and leave them all alone. Principal Nye reluctantly got on with her life, including taking another wife, and she resisted all attempts at evangelism by her former family and remained an obstinate heretic to the bitter end.

Maria Delgado was eventually released from prison, having served her time—like Allie, she hadn't been granted parole either—and she was reunited with her family. Mrs. Delgado did not get involved again with the underground railroad directly, but she still worked for the benefit of the unborn through her work as a political activist.

Mrs. Billie Jo McAllister retired from being a certified public accountant and enjoyed her retirement (or as much as she could enjoy it, given the current political climate).

General practitioner Laura Ward and registered diagnostic medical sonographer Daphne Cates continued to practice their respective disciplines of medicine at the Hennepin County Medical Center, while persisting in performing their covert operations of illegal ultrasounds for the benefit of pregnant women who entertained doubts about submitting to the abortion law (or, as the two ladies referred to it, the "No child left alive" policy). They had yet to be found out by the oppressive, progressive authorities.

Rodney J. McAllister, attorney-at-law, continued to work as legal counsel, representing defendants of the Christian faith (he even won a case occasionally).

Dr. Cynthia McAllister remained a drug counselor at the Hennepin County Drug Rehabilitation Clinic.

Jack Holtz secured employment at the rehab center (thanks to Dr. Cindy's assistance), and Allison Jane Holtz continued to work as her brother's legal secretary to help pay the bills.

Cynthia Josephine Holtz, having regained her facility for

the flute (following the deterioration of her musical skills due to her Euphoria addiction), obtained a place in the prestigious Minneapolis Philharmonic Orchestra while she was yet a high school sophomore. She even got to play on some songs whose lyrics she agreed with, though no lyrics were sung, as the orchestra only performed instrumental works—Bach and Handel still were perennial favorites.

At the ripe old age of fifteen (no longer just an emancipated teen but now considered a qualified adult), Jo finally gained a healthy amount of weight and, for a change, decided to wear her dark red hair on the short side. Her relations with her parents became far more harmonious, and the former child of disobedience became a dutiful daughter; she obeyed her parents, rather than the state.

Jo and her family and Taylor and the believing members of her family remained children of obedience because they obeyed the commandments of the Lord, who bought them and whom they loved.

Printed in the United States
By Bookmasters